BRUSHED BY BETRAYAL

BOOK TWO IN THE KAHUNA GROUP SERIES

L.A. SARTOR

1

THE WOMAN WHINED IN JADE LAURENT'S EAR. "YOU PROMISED ME the sapphire would be delivered today. The bank is going to close in an hour. Why can't you stand by your promises? Your father always did—"

"Evan has the Khan, Mrs. Cole. He's just been delayed." Jade counted to three, then four, frustrated by not only the haughty English accent Mrs. Elvina Cole layered on like treacle but by her phone calls every thirty minutes since noon—more annoying as Jade had already told her that Evan's flight hadn't been scheduled to arrive until 2 p.m. "I can't control traffic. I'm sure—"

"Don't interrupt me. I used to be treated like I was the most important client Laurent Art Brokers had. Now I don't even get a courtesy call or a car to pick me up and take me to the office. It's a ride-share or, heaven forbid, an American taxi."

True, Jade admitted to herself. Things had changed after her father died. She brushed aside the guilt Mrs. C was so good at inserting slyly into any conversation and focused on the real problem. It was just shy of four o'clock, and Evan should have been here by now. It was only an hour's drive from Denver International Airport.

It had been planned so that he had enough time to get to the office and have Mrs. Cole watch as Jade tested and inspected the famous and supposedly cursed sapphire. Then they'd have plenty of time to get Mrs. Cole to the bank. But traffic between DIA and Boulder was never predictable.

The haughty voice continued. "I don't know why you had Evan Fischer courier the Khan. I thought you were going to Singapore to handle it."

"Because this is what he does. He's a master at it. Dad trusted him implicitly, and Evan has done this for decades. It was stated in our contract, remember?"

"Hmph. So you say. I want you or Evan to drive me to the bank. That, too, was in our contract."

"Naturally. In fact, if this works for you, since time is short, we'll come to your house for the delivery and testing. Then we can take you immediately to the bank. I'll pack my equipment as soon as we hang up."

"And then you'll wait until I'm done to bring me home. Yes, I'll accept that. You call the minute you're on your way."

Jade looked to the ceiling as if the cream-colored plaster could offer her a snappy comeback. "Yes, of course," was all she managed, only to realize the line was dead. "Damn."

The door to her office opened and her best friend, Megan Rice, the woman who kept everything straight at Laurent Art Brokers, poked her head in. "Am I safe to enter? I saw the phone light go off, and knowing who you were talking to, I'm just being cautious in case you were going to throw the phone at the door."

Megan stepped into the office holding a crystal diffuser of her favorite lavender oil and put it on Jade's side of the partners' desk. "Too bad Mrs. Cole has the direct office line, so I can't stall her for you."

"Yeah, one of Dad's white-glove treatments for special clients." Jade air-quoted *special*. "How Dad stood her all those years is a mystery. And thank goodness she doesn't have my cell number. That was an excellent suggestion on your part."

Megan curtsied, holding out her forest green tunic with one hand, the other tucked behind her as if she were on stage.

Jade's buddy was taller than her own five-two by a few inches, but Megan still could be mistaken for a pixie, with her tumbled mass of fiery red curls and laughing blue eyes.

Holding up a finger to her lips, Jade feigned deep thought. "I wonder if we could fake a busy signal just for that line?"

"Greg would know how. I'll ask him when he gets back."

Jade knew better than to ask where Megan's fiancé, Greg Harrison, was now. The only thing Megan would be able to say is "on a stakeout." She never knew where or for how long. Meg had the tolerance level of a saint, but Jade could see past the mask of bravery and forbearance and knew her buddy was always worried when her fiancé was away. "Greg's a genius, so I have no doubt he could rig something like that. But seriously, the woman is a complete piece of work. I wonder if she's always been like that? I know her son loves her, but even he told me he can't tolerate her for long. I wish he were here now."

"Yes, she dotes on him. Too bad David Cole, son extraordinaire to quote his mum, lives in Hawaii. I'm sure he chose that spot for his tech biz on purpose. He can still live in the US yet be as far away as possible from 'Mother.'"

Jade nodded, completely agreeing with Megan. David was the antithesis of his prim and proper mother. She pictured him —dark blond hair on the longish side, serious blue eyes that could twinkle with a joke—and realized it was only late morning in Hawaii. When he was in town, they often got together and once had compared notes on what their typical day was like. She knew he'd already been out for a ride on the waves with his traditional longboard and would have finished his jog around his upscale Black Point neighborhood. By now David would be at work in a downtown Honolulu high rise that housed his booming tech biz. He'd gone from a simple laptop to a billion-dollar company with offices in four global centers of commerce, and he'd offered to show her any of the cities firsthand. Maybe that was exactly what she needed—a long vacation on the beach instead of sitting here, fending off an impatient client.

Megan pointed to the crystal diffuser she'd brought in. "Breathe. Now."

Holding the small container to her nose, Jade inhaled the calming scent deeply. "If this weren't the biggest commission I've done to date, I wouldn't have taken it, but the acquisition of the Khan will be, forgive me, the crown jewel of my tenure as head of Laurent Art Brokers."

Megan nodded, then looked like she wanted to say something about what this day honestly meant. Instead, she pirouetted and headed back to her domain, the main room of the business, closing the door softly behind her.

Grateful for Megan's reticence, Jade rubbed her temples. She wasn't particularly worried about Evan's late arrival, though an update text would have helped her cause with Mrs. Elvina Cole. And with such a beautiful early spring day she was sure the roads were filled with traffic. Still, he should have let her know he was delayed.

Letting loose a deep, from-the-heart sigh, Jade looked across the partners' desk to the vacant space. Nothing, not the biggest commission to date, not the amazing weather, not Evan's delayed arrival, could camouflage what this day really represented.

It was the one-year anniversary of her father's untimely death.

He died by a hit and run in the very parking lot of the building they owned, located near Boulder's Pearl Street Mall. His case was still open, but she knew it would now be nearly impossible for the perpetrator to be found and serve the sentence for his or her crime.

Getting up, she moved to her father's side of the desk and sat in his antique chair, hearing its springs creak. She picked up his pipe and inhaled the sweet scent still lingering in the burled wooden bowl, though it was growing fainter by the day.

Gerard Laurent's Hermès tweed jacket still hung on the Arts and Craft oak coat rack. The two comfortable leather chairs for clients, grouped with an old steamer trunk fashioned into a table, stood as vacant sentinels to his absence.

The emptiness of the inner sanctum, as her father called it, exacerbated the increasing discomfort she experienced over running the business alone. She hadn't taken the time to examine the root of the irritant. It wasn't running the business. She could handle it and its often demanding clients, even if she didn't like that schmoozing part of the business.

Maybe she was simply tired of the loneliness.

Jade picked at the dent her father had made in the cherry desk during a rare fit of anger, something she'd witnessed only once. She'd just entered their office and he was on the phone, gesturing wildly with his heavy antique brass paper opener. Then he slammed it on the desk, scattering the thick sheets of luxurious writing paper. Abruptly ending the call, he gathered the papers and stuffed them into his coat pocket. At her questioning look, he told her he'd be back later and left.

He was, but the next day security cameras were installed in the office and hall, alarms in both her and her father's home, and new security protocols for the building itself. Swipe cards for after hours and weekends and a camera in the elevator. It all seemed excessive to Jade, but no matter how much she pressed her father, he remained mute. As did their colleague, Evan Fischer.

Which brought her thoughts full circle.

She realized a huge amount of the frustration she was feeling with Mrs. Cole was really a reaction to the sad date. Jade had dreaded this day, knowing the wounds that were just beginning to scab were going to be torn open and tears would fall again.

The phone on her desk shrilled again and she simply ignored it.

How did you handle them, Dad? It isn't easy dealing with prima donna clients, yet you always smiled and charmed them.

Suddenly the tears fell hot and fast. Not moving or bothering to wipe them away, she let them fall, trying to breathe through the incredible pain of loss.

The door to her office opened again. In a flash she was out of her chair and wrapped in the arms of Megan.

She had no idea how long she stood there cocooned in the warm support of her best friend. The only sounds were of her own ragged pain. But slowly the tears stopped, and her breath came easier.

Jade stepped back and Megan pulled a tissue from her pocket, offering it to her. "Listen, I know you said you wanted to be alone tonight, but how about you come out to dinner with Malcolm and me? He's finishing up a case and we're celebrating."

Malcolm Talbot, the co-owner of Harrison & Talbot Investigations, was the only source of news about Megan's fiancé, Greg, who was on some stealthy, no personal contact job —somewhere.

Jade pegged Malcolm as the kind of guy who wouldn't appreciate having to cheer up a morose woman. She knew Megan adored him as a friend, but Malcolm's choice of women leaned toward the witty, stylish, and magazine cover-worthy. The exact opposite of Jade Laurent. Not that she wasn't stylish—she loved clothes, but she wasn't witty and certainly not cover-worthy.

She took the tissue Megan offered, wiped her face, then shook her head. "Thanks for the offer, but no. I'm betting that you want to pump Malcolm for information about Greg."

"There's nothing he'll tell me that you can't hear. So that excuse won't wash," Megan said, her arms now crossed.

Jade gave Megan a weak grin over her militant stance. "No, you two go, celebrate, get news on Greg. But I do think I'll head home if you can hold down the fort. I'll text Evan to come to the house, and we'll immediately head off to Mrs. C's. It's really as quick to get there from my home as it is from here."

Just then, the ring of bells indicated someone had entered the office.

"Evan," they exclaimed in unison and hurried to greet him.

Instead they found Smythe, an unremarkable man except for his talent at reproducing artists' work. He studied two periods intensely, allowing him to reproduce those works with impeccable detail. American Modernism with Georgia O'Keefe was his favorite artist and the Impressionist period with Mary Cassatt his top choice.

"Great, you're both here. I can't wait to show you how my latest commission turned out."

Jade bit back her groan and Megan plastered on a look of interest. Only Jade knew it was totally feigned.

Laurent Art Brokers had increasing numbers of wealthy clients across the world who paid top dollar for reproductions of their priceless original art to hang in their homes or offices while keeping their originals in a home or off-premises vault. In fact, the practice of hanging reproductions was becoming more common even for museum collections as thieves were becoming cleverer and artwork priceless.

Smythe, who had no first name they knew of, was as usual hunched over. Megan thought he seemed to have some sort of posture issue. His ratty, faded baseball cap was apparently a permanent feature, probably to cover his balding pate, even though he had a gray scraggly ponytail sticking out the back. And his eyes were magnified by thick glasses. In fact, he looked a bit like a hunched over old frog.

Yet he moved quickly, almost darting to the door as he hauled the large canvas backward, so the stretchers showed, as always refusing any help. "Ready?"

Jade's interest was real even though his timing was bad. After all, detecting forgeries was part of her specialty, and she loved the challenge—far more interesting than negotiating deals and soothing difficult customers.

The quality of Smythe's work had never let her down. He truly was one of the best reproduction artists in the world.

With a flourish, he whirled the painting around. It was a stunning reproduction of Georgia O'Keeffe's *Mariposa Lilies and Indian Paintbrush*, painted in 1941.

"May I?" Jade asked the man.

"I expect you to. It's your reputation on the line as well as mine."

But today it took more than a little effort for her to switch on her art-expertise mode. She carefully scanned the painting, noting that the strokes were perfect, the signature flawless. Then, looking at the back, she noted that even the wood stretchers holding the canvas were of the era's style and right age. Smythe was a perfectionist, and all the details mattered to him. A client or his "audience" wouldn't be able to tell whether the stretchers or the paint era were correct. All that mattered was that the client could show off their painting, confident in the knowledge their original was safe and secure.

Jade nodded. "Fine work. The clients will be incredibly happy. It would take a much closer examination, even infrared reflectography or mass spectrometry equipment, to detect this as a reproduction."

Smythe beamed. "I'll get it crated tonight and hopefully freighted tomorrow."

He carried out the painting, and Megan closed the door behind him. "Such a strange dude."

Jade nodded. "Another holdover from Dad."

And with that, her stomach roiled and her head swam. She extended her hand to steady herself, finding nothing to hold onto until Megan grabbed her.

"Listen, go home. Eat. I know you haven't had anything all day. Anyway, there is no way now that you'll make the bank in—"

As if on cue, the phone in Jade's office rang again. It could only be Mrs. Cole.

Jade shook her head at Megan's raised brow. "To be honest Meg, I don't know what to think about Evan. He always stays in touch and I have no news to tell Mrs. Cole."

The phone continued its shrill tone. Jade snatched up the receiver on Megan's desk and pushed the button for her private line. "Mrs. Cole, I haven't heard more from Evan, and we won't make it to the bank in time now. So I'm suggesting we meet early, here at the office just before the banks open. I'll send a car for you."

"You are an incredible disappointment to me, Jade Laurent."

"I'm sure I am, but there is nothing more I can do at the moment." And with that she replaced the receiver in its cradle.

"Go. I've got the office, and it's near closing time anyway," Megan said.

Jade didn't need another nudge. Bolting into her office, she gathered her phone, purse, and jacket, still fighting the queasiness roiling her stomach. She lifted a hand to Megan as she dashed through the reception area and left the suite. For a nanosecond she deliberated taking the elevator. Not relishing the stale air of the enclosure even for a brief time, she beat back the nausea and ran down the oak stairs of the two-story office building her father had built and she now owned.

The chill in the spring air did little to calm her stomach as she drove the short distance from downtown Boulder to Mapleton Hill and home.

THIS LAST CASE TOOK MORE OUT OF MALCOLM THAN HE'D thought possible. He was barely forty, yet right now he felt several decades older as he climbed the stairs to Laurent Art Brokers to pick up Megan for dinner.

Not only had his client withheld vital information, he'd lied. Perhaps the better description was *overstated his position*. Eventually, it came down to having a bit more than a heart-to-heart talk with the man, getting to the real issue and not just the grievance. It was done, the client happy, and the swindler facing a long string of indictments.

Malcolm shook off his feeling of dullness and stopped at the brass plaque denoting Megan's workplace. As per long-standing habit, he quickly surveyed the area. A discrete camera focused on the door and would show any visitor. A small buzzer was set into the framework. There was also a heavy brass knob, which he tried.

Locked.

He glanced at his watch, realizing it was a bit after five o'clock. He knew Megan was in. They'd texted not ten minutes ago. Pressing the buzzer, he smiled up at the camera. When the snick of locks opening sounded, he turned the knob and entered.

Megan held up one finger as she talked on the phone—more like grimacing than smiling, he noted, as he could hear a woman talking in loud emphatic tones with an English accent. While he waited, he took the time to glance around the large room and admired how it was cleverly divided into Megan's workspace and a foyer-sitting area, complete with coffee bar in a simple yet classic pecan armoire. Probably an antique, and he'd bet anything those were china cups for the clients. Various types of artwork graced the walls, but he didn't know a Picasso from a Renoir. No couches, but several armchairs that had high backs. Queen Anne, he thought he remembered hearing when he was touring a mansion at a charity gig.

His gaze moved to Megan's area of the office. Yep, it was all hers. A plank of stained teak atop black metal legs, a large laptop, phone, a tall stack of files, and the always-filled cup of coffee within easy reach.

Finally, she hung up the phone. "You look awful."

He grinned. Only Megan and Greg, his partner, would dare be that honest with him. "And you look a bit harried."

"It's been more than a trying day." She got up from behind her desk and he met her halfway, enfolding her in a hug. Three years ago, they'd briefly dated. Megan hadn't observed his unspoken rules regarding the way he conducted relationships. She'd call him for a picnic or a drive in the mountains and surprisingly he'd go with her. She frequently refused his invitations if they involved going to the latest opening or gala.

Megan listened instead of talked and soon he'd opened up to her as he'd never done with a woman before. They became friends instead of lovers. Then he introduced her to his partner, Greg Harrison.

Shortly, Malcolm was going to be best man at their July wedding.

Now, as he smiled in sympathy, she pointed at the phone and rolled her eyes. "That was a client who has been a pain in the patootie from day one. Long before Jade was the remaining Laurent of Laurent Art Brokers. And worse, today is the anniversary of Jade's father's accident."

Malcolm had heard all about that hit and run and done some digging on his own, but the trail went cold almost immediately. And he knew all too well how these sad anniversaries seemed to take one by surprise and bring up all sorts of memories. Eventually one could remember with less intensity. But he knew from experience that to reach that point usually took longer than 365 days. "Do you want to call off our dinner and be with Jade?"

"Thanks for offering. I already suggested she have dinner with us, knowing you wouldn't really mind. But she refused. So let's go out, you can tell me about Greg, and we can share an expensive bottle of wine, your treat. Then once I have you mellowed out, you'll feel like telling me if you're ready to cut back a bit."

"The wine sounds great, as does a dinner with my favorite girl, but I can answer your question right now. Yes, I need a break of some sort. With no vacations, no breaks in case load for the past fifteen years, I think I need a change of scenery. Once you and Greg get back from your honeymoon, I'll figure it out."

"Finally. Let's start figuring it out tonight. Just let me finish making a note in Mrs. Cole's file and put everything away."

A singsong note chimed from her computer. Returning to her desk she glanced at the camera view of the door. "Hmmm, I don't recognize them. Let's wait until they leave, and then you can buy that really great bottle of Cabernet, okay?"

MEGAN'S WORDS IMMEDIATELY DROVE HIM TO LOOK AT HER computer screen. Malcolm was overly cautious, to the point of annoyance according to Megan, but it didn't matter. It's what he did.

He recognized the two men on the monitor and their presence never signified good news. "That's odd."

They stood at the office door, looking up at the camera as he had minutes ago. As usual, Tomba was rocking on his heels.

"Malcolm?"

"Meg, I know them. They're police detectives. There is no reason why these guys should show up here unless it's something new about Gerard's death. Maybe they found a lead. You should let them in."

As Megan scanned his face with a question on hers, he simply nodded, hiding his unease. This was Denver PD at the door, not Boulder PD who should be handling the case.

She pressed the button to unlock the door, and the two men in street clothes with jackets likely concealing their weapons entered the office. Then they stopped in their tracks.

"Talbot, what are you doing here?"

"Why is Denver Homicide here?" Malcolm countered.

"Denver Homicide?" Megan echoed.

"We need to talk to a Jade Laurent. There is no home address for her, or phone number. We got this address off—"

He shut up as if saying too much.

"She's home." Megan's voice quivered just a bit.

"It's vital we talk with her tonight," the heavier of the two said. "Who are you?" he asked, looking at Megan.

Malcolm shook his head in mock dismay. "Meg, these guys, who really are nicer than they're behaving, are Tomba, the one who asked the question, and Moore, the nicer one. Don't let them scare you."

"Megan Rice, assistant to Jade Laurent *and* her best friend. Is this about her father's death?"

"No, ma'am."

"Ah, see, you got a 'ma'am.'" Malcolm tried to lighten the atmosphere.

"She'll be here in the morning," Megan offered.

"This really can't wait until then."

Malcolm met Meg's glance, which told him that she wanted to be around if Tomba and Moore were going to Jade's house. And whatever the issue was sounded serious enough that they needed to go tonight. "We'll meet you there. Do not go to the door until we're with you, as a courtesy to me."

Moore nodded. "We owe you that."

Only then did Megan write Jade's address on a piece of paper and hand it to Moore.

FINALLY JADE HEARD THE SHORT RIFT OF CAROLE KING ON HER phone. Evan was at the door. She didn't try and hide the tear tracks on her cheeks. Evan would understand better than anyone. In fact, she needed to see him, to share this moment with him. She knew he missed Gerard Laurent as much as she did.

Untangling from the afghan she'd wrapped around herself, she jumped off the couch and swiftly opened the door, only remembering at the last moment she was supposed to check the camera monitor on her phone. A lesson her dad tried to instill, but one that apparently never took hold.

Instead of Evan, an anxious Megan and an unsmiling Malcolm stood there along with two unfriendly-looking men behind them. Scanning her buddy's anxious face, Jade's stomach dropped. "Meg, what's wrong? Oh my God, is it Greg? Is he okay?" She clutched her friend's arm.

"No, it's not Greg—"

"May we come in?" Malcolm asked.

Jade glanced at him, then back at Megan, who nodded. She didn't believe Malcolm would bring anyone to her home who wasn't vetted by him, but who were those men and why was Megan involved?

The man next to Megan answered her unspoken question. "Detectives Tomba and"—he nodded toward the second man— "Moore." Jade's heart skipped a beat. Police? She opened the door wide to let them in, trying to slow the sudden acceleration in her breathing. Leading the way into her dimly lit living room, she turned on a few lamps as she passed.

Once all five of them crowded inside the small room, it felt claustrophobic, so she moved to stand in front of the fireplace. She glanced at the couch, realizing her afghan was bunched up, taking up most of the room on the Ultrasuede cushions. Crossing to the couch, she picked up the still-warm throw and methodically folded it, then tucked it inside the ottoman, a gesture she made only to calm herself. The wine bottle and glass could stay right where they were, but now people could sit.

Nobody did. They were apparently waiting until she stopped fluttering around.

Taking several slow, deep breaths, hoping they might soothe her, also failed. She hid her shaking hands in the pockets of the fleece tunic she wore. This visit was reminiscent of the police coming to tell her of her father's "accident." In fact, that was probably the very reason they were here, to shed new light on the investigation. Finally.

But then why were Megan and Malcolm also here?

The ticking of the clock on the mantel behind her seemed to pound its rhythm into her ears.

"You are Jade Laurent?"

"I am, and you are?" She couldn't recall either of their names.

"Detective Tomba from Denver Homicide." He repeated his name as he pulled a leather case out of his jacket pocket and flipped it open to reveal his shield.

She didn't glance at it, knowing since Malcolm was here, they were who they said. "Denver? Have you found a new lead in my father's accident?"

"No, ma'am. Detective Moore." The smaller man introduced himself and did the same routine with his shield. He then removed a small folio from his upper pocket and withdrew a glassine envelope, handing it to her. "Does this belong to you?"

Fighting the disappointment that these men offered her nothing more on her father's investigation, it took her a moment to register that the envelope held a Laurent Art Broker's business card. "It's a card for my business."

Megan moved to stand beside her and, as Jade scanned her buddy's face, she saw her friend nod toward Malcolm. Jade got the message that she wasn't alone in whatever this was about. Their support gave her a small measure of courage.

"Do you usually have business cards without names on them?" The bigger detective asked.

That was an odd question. "Yes, I have my cards. Meg," she nodded toward her friend, "has cards with her name on them. And we have blank cards. It's standard procedure in our business."

"Can you recognize the writing on the back?" Detective Moore asked.

Jade turned over the envelope to read aloud, "Please let Jade Laurent know she's next and the clock has ticked down to now.

Then the circle will be complete." The black writing slashed across the card's cream-colored surface was in stark contrast with the polite wording of the message.

Megan's gasp mirrored her own shock.

Jade thrust the card back at the detective as Malcolm moved forward with hand outstretched for it.

"Denver Homicide? Where did you find that?" She pointed to the packet Malcolm now held.

"At the scene of a death."

Evan? No, no! But who else could it be? Jade's knees buckled and had Malcolm not moved quickly and grasped her elbow, she'd have fallen to the floor. He manhandled her to the couch, and she barely made it as blackness narrowed her vision.

"Keep your head down," Malcolm directed as he pressed her shoulders forward. "Meg, water?"

Moments later, a finger raised her chin and an opened bottle of water was put to her lips.

"Can you drink some?"

Jade managed a small sip.

"Another," he ordered.

She did as commanded, then tried to form words. "Where?"

"Late this afternoon, a gentleman was found in the restroom of Denver International Airport. This was near the body, er, person."

"Did you ID the ..."

"No ma'am. There was no identification on him."

It couldn't be Evan. Impossible.

But he hasn't called or texted since the plane touched down. That's so unlike him. He'd know I would worry.

"Was there a prosthesis for his right arm?"

"We're not allowed to touch the body to check other than to see if the victim is alive. The coroner will have that information."

A tiny flame of hope ignited deep inside her.

"Ma'am, your business card was on the floor, next to the body. We need a positive ID."

"Tomba, can't this wait until morning?" Malcolm asked in sharp tones.

"No, Talbot, it can't. The coroner has requested that a forensic pathologist conduct an autopsy. It was an unattended death, and then there was that note on the back of the business card."

Then the words in the message hit her. The card said *next.* Was it a threat? Was *she* next?

Dimly through the haze of fear of what she'd find at the coroner's office and the note's threat, she felt the warmth of Malcom's hand on her shoulder, offering support.

The thinner detective kneeled by Jade. "We need you to come with us to the Denver medical examiner's office—tonight."

A sob came from Megan's direction. She looked to find her friend's fist pressed against her lips, trying to hold back her emotion.

Jade reached out a shaking hand to her, and Meg moved over to grasp it, her hand as icy as her own. "It's possible it's not Evan, Meg. It's still possible."

"You're not going alone, Jade. I'm coming too." Meg sniffled.

"I'll bring them both," Malcolm offered.

2

JADE, FLANKED BY MALCOLM AND MEGAN, STOOD AT THE SIDE OF the stainless table in the cold, horribly utilitarian and soulless room.

Bright lights flooded the wide, wheeled gurney holding a draped body.

Hope against hope flared in Jade. That this wasn't Evan, but rather a horrible mistake.

Dr. Mendez, Denver's chief medical examiner and forensic pathologist, waited patiently for her nod before pulling back the drape.

Megan's fingers touched hers, then held tightly as Jade nodded once, and the drape was drawn down to reveal a face.

Her wish wasn't granted.

She stared down at her mentor and her father's best friend. For as long as she could remember, Evan had been the one to keep everyone on schedule. If Dad had been tied up with a client, Evan made sure she got to her piano lessons on time, her homework was done, and she ate dinner. And though Evan wasn't technically a partner in the business, he'd helped her father build a prestigious art brokering business—a business both men had tutored her to take over some day.

Now both men were gone.

"It is Evan Fischer," Jade said, her throat thick with grief.

Megan's eyes widened in disbelief. "That's not Evan—what are you talking about?"

Jade dimly realized her friend had released her hand and backed a few paces away from the table. She wished she could do the same. "Megan, believe me. It is Evan."

A deep sob came from Megan, sounding as far away as the moon.

Dr. Mendez talked into the microphone above the gurney. "Jade Laurent has visually identified Evan Fischer. Fingerprints of his left hand have been forwarded to the Denver Police lab. The right prosthesis has been removed."

"This is being recorded?" Jade asked.

"Yes."

"Video?"

"No. Not at the moment."

"Then I'll explain so the recorder has this." Jade heard her voice—it sounded robotic. Nevertheless, she wanted this all on record. Unlike her father's murderer, Evan's would be brought to justice, and she wanted nothing to hinder that process.

"His mustache is applied, his tan is fake, and I'm sure you've noticed his teeth? He would use some sort of prosthetic to change his mouth and cheek structure. And his silver hair color isn't real, it's usually brown. He probably has contacts in, as he normally needs glasses. His eye color is brown. Was his passport found with him?"

"No, there was nothing but the business card."

She drew a ragged breath. "Could I see his right arm please?" If his death was the result of someone stealing the Khan, she'd better know right this minute. She'd deal with the crushing guilt later.

"It is a prosthesis, and I have removed it from Mr. Fischer," Albert Mendez cautioned in a gentle tone.

Perhaps he was trying to spare her, but she didn't need patience or caution, she needed answers. "Yes, I know. I need to see his arm." Jade didn't want to explain right now, she just needed to verify for herself that she was totally at fault for his death. That the cursed and famous Kublai Khan had brought death on yet another person.

Dr. Mendez reached under the drape and brought out Evan's prothesis. He laid it on the gurney's edge.

Jade sucked in air, stunned. "Impossible."

"What?" Malcolm asked.

"His arm. It hasn't been tampered with."

"Jade?"

Megan sounded as puzzled as Jade felt. "Evan couriered small objects in his arm."

"What kind of objects?"

She heard the suspicion in Dr. Mendez's voice and couldn't blame him. However, she needed him to be on her side. And sadly, there was no reason for this to remain secret any longer.

"Not drugs. I own an art brokering company. Evan would courier small objects like jewelry or gems, even small carvings in his arm. Safer than traveling with a briefcase that could be snatched. Nearly invisible and known to only a few people."

Megan moved back to stand beside her. Jade's gaze swung from Megan to Malcolm, expecting to see skepticism. Instead, sorrow laced with support showed on their faces.

She deeply appreciated it, but the guilt enveloping her snugged tighter. If they only knew she'd sent Evan on a journey he'd warned her against. She'd been stubborn to the point where she said she'd undertake the trip herself if he didn't.

He did, and his life ended.

All because she believed this huge commission could establish her as the true heir to Laurent Art Brokers. She had to know the truth—and what the hell that message meant scrawled on the back of the card. *Next?* How? Why?

There was only one more step to finding part of the answers. "May I? I'll only need to touch his finger and the watch."

"Then please put on gloves." Dr. Mendez reached behind him to a table holding instruments, then held out a pair of stretchy gloves.

Fumbling at first, she finally pulled them on so she could do what was needed. She glanced over at Dr. Mendez.

He nodded his approval for her to proceed.

Tamping down her dread, Jade recited her actions for the recorder as she made them. Setting Evan's old Timex watch to 2:30, she then pulled his prosthetic little finger. A small rectangle sprang open in the prosthesis's forearm. She stepped back. "I believe you'll find there is a pouch nestled inside."

The ME looked into the small space as Jade waited for him to pull out the small bag holding the famous and nearly priceless Kublai Khan sapphire.

"It's empty."

MALCOLM SAW HER STARE AT DR. MENDEZ WITH DISBELIEF.

"Impossible. Evan texted me that he'd acquired it and was coming home," Jade exclaimed.

"Yet you said the prosthesis hadn't been tampered with," Malcolm countered. He didn't want to press her, but he was also aware that a solid voice recording of all that they saw was vital for the prosecution when they found the murderer.

"Yes, at least not by him, and had it been someone else, the flap wouldn't have closed. Look, I'll show you." She moved back to the gurney and with her gloved finger, she pressed on the door, trying again with three fingers and a bit more force. "The door won't close."

"What was the purpose behind this?"

Jade shook her head. "I just know there was a reset. I don't know what or how or why. I'm sure Dad knew."

Malcolm noted her fortitude was nearly spent. Jade could barely get the words out through colorless lips. Her green eyes held confusion and pain. He didn't want to add to it. Nevertheless, his investigative instincts wouldn't let him stop asking questions. "It may have been created for exactly this circumstance. What was he couriering for you?"

"The Kublai Khan. A famous pear-shaped sapphire worth millions. You know he was leaving for Tuscany next week. To accept a shipment of furniture for his new villa. He was healthy, probably healthier than me. He'd recently had a heart scan to prove it, telling me *I* needed more exercise. Now he's dead. Most likely murdered."

The room was silent for several heart beats. Jade was rambling, and Malcolm knew that wasn't unexpected with this kind of shock.

"I'll turn off the microphone now," Dr. Mendez stated for the record.

Malcolm nodded to the ME, who had taken a step back from the gurney but remained watchful. As he should. However, the distance was enough to give a modicum of privacy. Malcolm appreciated the man's tact and would thank him later. Albert Mendez was a top-notch forensic pathologist and had earned his title of Chief Medical Examiner with his tenacity and skill. They'd worked together on other cases and over late-night beers had swapped some life stories including their love of solving crimes. Each in his own way.

Not knowing a better time to say this, Malcolm gently cupped Jade's chin, turning it up so she had to look away from Evan's body. "Jade, it's worse than just the horror of Evan's death and the missing stone. You're now a target." He waited a beat for that to sink in. "The best thing to do is get you to a safe house for at least tonight, but most likely longer. The firm has a couple we use for clients. And if you want, I have two investigators that are available to take on this case right away."

Color began to bloom on Jade's cheeks, replacing the chalky white of the last few hours. A spark of stubbornness flashed in her green eyes. She stepped back, breaking the gentle hold he had on her chin.

"I'm not hiding in a safe house. Evan is dead, the Khan is missing, and I have a big fat X on my back. Everything my father and Evan built is in jeopardy, and you expect me to hide?"

Malcolm hadn't expected refusal. "You're not going to have a legacy at all if you're dead," he countered ruthlessly in a tone that worked on countless numbers of clients who could be foolish.

Megan's gasp was the only sound in the room.

Jade looked away, and he knew he had her.

Until she bent over and kissed Evan's cheek a final time, then nodded to the ME and Megan and headed for the door.

Surprised, Malcolm glared after her, noting her rigid posture.

"Compromise, doofus. Say something," Megan hissed at him.

He glared at her, then softened as tears filled her eyes. This was about Jade, her best friend, he reminded himself.

"Jade," he called just as she reached the door. "Leaving won't protect you or find Evan's killer."

That stopped her. She turned and walked right to him, standing toe to toe. He studied her face, pinched with exhaustion and sorrow, yet that small flame he'd seen in her eyes had grown into full-fledged determination.

"I'll make a deal with you. I'll go to your 'safe place' for tonight, although I *do* have security at my own home. And I accept your offer to have someone you trust work on this case. But I help."

Malcolm let out a sharp bark of laughter. "That's not a deal, that's an ultimatum. And a poor one. What special skills do you have to protect yourself? Are you an expert shot? Black belt?"

He felt the jab of Megan's sharp elbow in his back and stepped far enough away for her to squeeze in between them. She topped Jade's height by several inches, but that wasn't saying much as he guessed Jade was around five-two. Nevertheless, Malcolm knew size had never stopped Meg from anything she'd put her mind to. She mussed her red curls as she ran her fingers through them. Malcolm nearly smiled, but he knew what was coming next as the fire of battle lit her blue eyes. Wisely, he took another step back. He'd seen that fire all too many times.

"You two are acting like petulant children. Stop it." She pivoted to Jade, and Malcolm felt a twinge of pity for her.

"Jade, I don't know why Evan is made up as he is. But he's dead. D-E-A-D," she emphatically spelled out. "So is your father and their best friend, Omarr. Something isn't right. Listen to macho man here—don't be pigheaded. I'm not going to another funeral after Evan's. Understand?"

Malcolm barely stifled his astonishment while Jade simply blinked. Megan turned on him. "Don't blow this." With that final word, she stepped back, glaring at them.

Jade sagged at Megan's burst of words. "Meg, you know I have security at my house. But for tonight … I'm okay with this."

Malcolm heard the utter fatigue lacing each word and made a snap decision. No sterile safe house for her. "Okay then.

Instead of the safe house, which is across town, we'll use my condo for tonight. Meg, you want to come as well?" She knew his digs as well as he knew the cabin where she and Greg lived. Greg used his place if he needed to stay in Denver to work, and they'd had many a drink and dinner prepared by Meg in Malcolm's huge kitchen.

Meg shook her head. "Thanks. I'll catch a rideshare back to my cabin."

"I'll have Mike drive you. He's waiting outside. I already set it up with him to get you both home when we were done here. Slight change in the number of passengers, but he's driving you home."

"Malcolm, I'm a big girl. I'll be fine."

Furrowing his brow, he stared sternly at her. "You could be used as bait, so no rideshare, not tonight, big girl. I know your cabin is secure, but Mike will see that you get there and escort you inside. Okay?"

Mike, his best protection agent, would be perfect for Jade's security after tonight.

Meg nodded and he felt better. Tomorrow he'd set stricter guidelines, but tonight he needed to think, and that required zero worry. Meaning Jade and Meg had to be secure.

"Wait, back up a minute," Jade said. "Your condo?"

"My condo is only blocks from here and fully rigged for security. There are three bedrooms. You can have any of them but mine."

3

In his Range Rover, Malcolm made the trip from the medical examiner's office to his condo in less than five minutes, surprising her. At this time of night there was practically no traffic and he missed all the lights.

"This is it," he said as he turned the corner and immediately wheeled onto the ramp leading to the massive subterranean garage.

She took it all in as they waited for the door to lift, looking up at the tall building, noting its soft red sandstone color, similar to the flatirons in Boulder and the red rocks around Golden. For some reason, it pleased her that Malcolm's place was not the cold gray of plain urban cement. Even though the building was cloaked in the dark of night, the lights in the various condos revealed a nod toward Prairie School architecture while blending into the big city. Jade knew Evan would have appreciated her assessment. A building's aesthetics were as essential as its functionality, and he'd always prodded her imagination by asking her why something worked or didn't. He considered architecture the physical manifestation of art.

Malcolm pulled into the garage, and she noticed he watched

in the rearview mirror as the huge, automated garage door closed behind them. The parking garage was brightly lit and completely utilitarian. Malcolm used a swipe card at the elevator and the door whispered open and then shut as quietly behind them. She noticed there were no buttons on the elevator, so his swipe card must be programmed for his floor.

Moments later, the door opened and Malcolm ushered her out of the elevator and down the carpeted hallway with his hand resting lightly on the small of her back.

Apparently, there was only one door on the floor. "Does each floor only have one unit?"

"In this tower. The other buildings in the complex are shorter and have three units on each floor."

There was unmistakable pride in his voice, leaving Jade with little doubt this must have cost him a pretty penny. Megan never mentioned anything about how successful Harrison & Talbot were, but now Jade had her answer.

Windows lined the other side of the corridor. And though it was well lit and high enough in the sky that nearby buildings' residents couldn't spy in, Jade moved a bit closer to Malcolm, feeling vulnerable.

Uneasy, she couldn't wait to get safely inside. But instead of unlocking the door, he pressed a spot on the door's molding, and a small panel slid open. Damn, another secret compartment, though far different from Evan's.

Puzzled, she watched him press his face to something for a second or two. "What are you doing?"

"Retinal scan."

"Seriously? You have clients so important that they need to be protected like this?"

"Nope. Just a nerd-crazy partner who loves all things high tech."

"You're James Bond to Greg's Q. Though I think you're more

detective than spy." She tried for a light tone, failing miserably. Too much had happened to keep pretending she wasn't scared spitless.

And yet one corner of his mouth lifted slightly, as if he liked her comparisons. "Oh, I carry a gun too."

"I don't carry a gun, and my home security system isn't as fancy, but it will serve."

"We'll fix that tomorrow."

It sounded to her like he was thinking of allowing her to be in her own house. Maybe she'd gotten through to him that she was capable of helping, somehow.

Yet, when he pushed open the door, she darted into his space, relieved to be away from the glass-walled corridor highlighting the target on her back.

She turned to survey the room, expecting a cold techno-geek environment in keeping with the fact this was a high rise in the heart of the newly revitalized neighborhood of LoDo, near the Denver Rockies stadium. And more so that he was a guy.

Instead, a deep pile carpet in rich espresso caressed her ankles. The fire in the granite fireplace flamed magically to life and looked like it was burning in cracked ice. And the view? Oh. My. Goodness. Worth any amount of money. The Denver skyline never looked so brilliant and alive.

Counterpoint to the emptiness of her heart.

"Retinal scan and scan cards, not very welcoming for dates, huh?" she joked feebly again, trying to push away the darkness if only for a second.

"I don't bring dates here."

Well, that was news. Headline news. Playboy Detective doesn't use bachelor pad. Malcolm was often pictured on social media squiring amazing-looking women to numerous fancy events. Those were the kinds of parties Jade avoided whenever she could. And something her father had adored attending.

"Shame," she murmured.

"What?"

She shook her head, but it truly was a shame that Malcolm's dates didn't get a look at this. Casually elegant, easy to live in and enjoy. Leather, wood, glass, and granite. Earth tones that cradled the body and spirit.

Just not hers at the moment.

"Pick your room. Mine is the first door on the right as you head down the hall. You need sleep for tomorrow."

Knowing he was right, but also knowing her fatigue wouldn't be cured by sleep, Jade headed in the direction he indicated. Then, as her brain engaged, she hastily retraced her steps. Malcolm was already seated in front of a computer and chair that had been hidden in the wall near the kitchen. He didn't turn around but obviously heard her.

"Need something?"

"Spare T-shirt, toothbrush, eye makeup remover." The last item got his attention.

He rose swiftly, and the computer getup folded back into the wall as he stepped away.

"That's a great trick."

"Again, Greg. He has one too. In fact, we've installed a number of these in people's houses. If they have to leave in a hurry, then everything is automatically tucked away. Like a safe room for a computer."

Jade knew Megan's fiancé was the geek side of Harrison & Talbot Investigations, but she'd never seen any of his work. Now twice in the space of a few minutes, she'd glimpsed his talent.

Following Malcolm as he headed for his bedroom, she hesitated outside the door, mildly curious about the room, but uncomfortable about entering.

"Got the toothbrush and even toothpaste but clean out of

eye gunk remover. Come, grab this, will you, and pick out a shirt you think will work."

She entered, stunned by the room. The king size bed didn't begin to fill the space, which was at least the size of the living room. A fire glittered in this room as well, its flickers muted by the suede-papered walls.

Jade followed his voice into a huge—no cavernous—closet. She loved her house, but this closet might be worth moving for. And it was completely organized by color and style. Sheesh, the man had to have domestic help.

The thought brought her full circle. Evan had died helping her. Tears welled up. She fought them down, wanting to grieve in private.

A sob erupted from deep in her soul.

MALCOLM HEARD JADE'S SOB AND TURNED TO SEE A BRAVE, STRONG woman breaking down. Her shoulders heaved, her face glimmered with tears, and her legs wobbled.

Knowing they wouldn't hold her another minute, he dropped everything and gathered her close as he lowered her to the bench in the closet.

Holding her tight, he felt her shudders as she fought for breath between the sobs. Rocking her gently, he let the storm play out until she was still against him.

He moved gingerly, checking to see if she'd fallen asleep after her outpouring of grief, only to see her staring at something he couldn't see or fathom.

The pain of loss wasn't something he could empathize with. When his father had died, Malcolm hadn't responded like this. And his mother? He'd been too young, only remembering that his father wasn't the same after Mom died.

His brothers had taken Dad's passing harder. At times they'd been okay, and other times, they'd gotten angry, sad, and then angry again. With no warning the emotions would just pour out.

Regardless of how one handled it, death was final.

And the woman he held was a target.

Picking up petite Jade took little effort. He carried her to the bedroom next to his and laid her gently on the coverlet. As he turned, her cold hand grabbed his wrist.

He understood her need. "I'll be right back, promise."

She released him, and he glimpsed a haunting emptiness in her eyes before they closed. Then he moved swiftly to his closet, gathering the left-behind T-shirt, toothbrush, toothpaste, and on impulse, snagged the comforter off his bed.

Jade wasn't asleep, her breathing more ragged than slow breaths. Malcolm placed the comforter over her and laid the necessities she'd requested at the foot of the bed.

He sat in the club chair closest to the bed. He couldn't leave her until she slept. If she slept.

Malcolm often pulled all-nighters and was prepared to do so tonight. But in less than an hour, Jade's breathing was even. He knew tomorrow would bring back the horror and loss but was grateful she had at least this time to let her body, if not her soul, recover from the shock.

After moving back to his own bedroom and stretching out on the bed, he attempted to stay alert but fell asleep, only to be jerked awake as he heard her soft footsteps. He checked the clock. 2 a.m.

He waited until she'd passed his room, then, stealthy as a panther, rose and followed her. Hidden in the shadow of the entry hall, he studied her, seated on the carpet in front of the flames, her knees pulled up under her chin, arms wrapped around them, wearing the heavy T-shirt he'd left on her bed. She appeared to be simply staring into the fire, radiating a deep melancholy. One that no words of his could ease.

Something primal stirred deep in his gut. An instinct to protect. Not because he was paid to do so, but because he needed to. Maybe he should break his own rule and be her protector instead of turning her over to his protection team. He'd already more or less acquiesced to allowing her to be in her own home by agreeing to update the security there.

Somehow putting someone else in charge of her 24-hour protection felt wrong. Safe, but wrong.

Padding quietly back to his room, he stood at the picture window, allowing the lights of the city to ease his unsettling emotional surge.

And just to reinforce his decision, he texted his assistant Shelley with instructions to clear Mike's schedule and prepare to move to Boulder as bodyguard to Ms. Jade Laurent. He'd make that one concession to their "agreement." Her house, but with Mike guarding her. And she wasn't helping investigate. Period.

Feeling steady and calm, knowing he was making the right decision to have his team do their thing while he did what he was good at, he spent the time researching Laurent Art Brokers, Gerard and Jade Laurent, and Evan Fischer while he waited until Jade returned to her room.

Jade had little social presence. A quick search revealed she'd earned two advanced degrees, one from the École Beaux-Arts de Paris and one from the Gemological Institute of America.

Evan had zero social presence, and little came up on a search for his past. Odd.

Gerard, on the other hand, had been quite the socializer. He didn't have media accounts but apparently didn't need them as news outlets photographed him with some of his most high-profile clients. He worked with the rich and famous. So Jade should have it made as far as keeping Laurent Art Brokers viable.

The murder was horrendous and the stone's loss indeed a blow, but he couldn't see how that would ruin her business. In fact, with the contrariness of public opinion, sadly, it might make her more appealing ... an urban legend. And none of this was her fault. How could it be?

Next, he emailed Albert Mendez and asked if, once cause of death was determined, it would be possible to let him know. Malcolm hadn't seen any wounds on Evan, at least on the head and neck areas. And he knew Albert would run tox screens, so he would hopefully know more soon.

In closing, Malcolm also mentioned that he was working for Jade. As he pressed Send, he heard Jade head back to her room and glanced at his phone clock. 4 a.m. She'd sat there for two hours. He wished he'd insisted that Megan stay at the condo as well. She'd know what to say to her best friend.

Dawn began to lighten the eastern spring sky. Too late to grab some deep shut-eye, so instead he headed to the kitchen and turned on his coffee machine. It whirred as it ground beans and steamed fresh hot coffee into his cup. The pungent scent helped him shake off the uncomfortable thought that perhaps Jade wouldn't see his solution as brilliant.

She said she wanted to help find the killer. Well, she couldn't. On that point he wouldn't compromise.

Right Talbot. And just what is *your compromise?*

Mike.

Right. Don't think Jade will see it that way.

Trying to shake off his persistent inner voice, he strode down the hall to Jade's room to tell her, only to see her breathing was now soft and even. There was no reason to wake her. He was simply in his usual get-it-done mode. Taking a step back mentally and figuratively, Malcolm let her sleep, knowing reality would hit hard the moment she woke.

SITTING ON A HIGH STOOL AT THE KITCHEN'S MARBLE COUNTER, Jade stared into the pottery mug she held with both hands.

"Do you need something else to doctor it up? Cream, sugar?"

She looked up from the mug at Malcolm, realizing she'd been sitting there for who knows how long, doing nothing. She couldn't even recall what she'd been thinking about.

Trying to pull herself up from the pit of emotion she was drowning in, she took a sip and shook her head. "No, it's fine. Thanks for making it."

"I'm guessing you're not hungry."

"You guessed right, but please, go ahead and fix what you want."

"I had a banana and granola bar with my first cup, so I'm okay for now. We need to go over my plans for you—"

"You truly aren't meaning for me to be locked up in a safe house with you guarding me, are you?"

"No—"

"Good, because while you may be a bodyguard and a hotshot investigator, you can't be both."

"Right, I'm just a hotshot investigator. And I've decided that instead of a safe house, we'll use yours, beef up the security as I mentioned last night, and have Mike, my number one personal protection agent, stay there with you."

Jade stiffened at his "I've decided," then as he finished the sentence, she realized he was compromising. A small glow of comfort helped ease the unnerving fact that she needed to have protection.

Under normal circumstances, Jade needed no man's strength

or coddling and had often resented her father's and Evan's over-protectiveness. What she wouldn't give for a word, any word, from either of them now.

And she realized Malcolm had said nothing about her being involved, helping find the sick person who'd killed Evan and wanted her dead as well.

She'd let it drop for the moment, not feeling up to figuring out how she'd convince him that she needed to do this. Must do this. For Evan. And for her own conscience.

"If you're ready, let's get a move on to your house. My building's garage is monitored, but just in case, if I give you a command, do it. Don't ask questions. Got it?"

Jade nodded once, her small ember of comfort gone, his words a horrible reminder that she had an X on her back.

THANKFULLY, MALCOLM GOT THEM OUT OF THE GARAGE WITHOUT incident, so there had been no reason to bark commands at Jade. While he was fairly sure she'd obey them without question, he wouldn't know for sure until the moment arose. After all, she wasn't a team member, hadn't been tested in the field under life-threatening circumstances.

He just didn't know how she'd react.

Even this early in the morning, traffic on I-25 to the Boulder turnoff was congested with commuters and trucks. Uptight drivers honked and gestured rudely as he weaved in and out of packed lanes, sped up and slowed down, all the while constantly vigilant. He watched for a tail and a way out if someone tried to box them in and then shoot them and run.

If it came down to a fight, Malcolm had a weapon. His concealed-carry 9mm Glock, usually worn in his waist holster, now rested in its specially designed holster nestled between the console and his seat.

Malcolm finally got his chance to pull ahead of the traffic mess. He punched the Range Rover and pulled sharply into the left lane to pass a triple-trailer semi lumbering in the center lane. He cleared the truck in nothing flat and was pulling back into the safer center lane when a distinctive red and white Ducati motorcycle, apparently hidden by the massive freight truck until now, zoomed from the right lane, swerved across two lanes, and slowed down in front of him. Malcolm slammed on his brakes.

He was boxed in, despite his precautions. "Damn."

Swiftly looking at Jade to gauge her reaction, he noted she was a shade paler if that was possible and was white-knuckling the arm rests.

Slipping his hand down the side of the seat, he pulled up the Glock and rested it on his lap.

"You think this was deliberate?"

Not taking his eyes off the biker in front of him, Malcolm motioned with his chin toward it. "He's watching us. See the slight swivel of his helmet as he turns to look in his sideview mirror?"

"Yes."

"If I tell you to duck, do it."

The distance between them and the bike was constant, slowing down or speeding up as Malcolm did. This cat and mouse game continued until they approached the exit to Boulder.

The biker gave a two-fingered salute to his helmet and gunned the powerful bike, slipping through cars and lanes like a pro.

Malcolm headed up the sharply curved ramp to US 36,

moving fast, furious at both himself and the traffic. "Who do you know that owns a Ducati bike."

"No one. And there wasn't a license."

"I noticed."

That was the last of any conversation until he pulled to the curb in front of a small 1900s' bungalow.

Jade let out a deep sigh. "Home. What did you do, memorize the address?"

"Yep, and the directions. I couldn't be distracted by using the GPS, and I didn't want to concentrate on spoken directions."

"Aren't we going in?"

"In a moment." He let the Range Rover idle as he scanned the area. The few other cars in the neighborhood appeared empty, and none had engines running. And as it was early spring, the trees were leafless, making the view clearer. Unfortunately, there was a tall fence on the north side of her cobbled driveway.

"Who lives over there?" He pointed to the fenced property.

"A retired couple. She was a pediatrician and he was a professor at the University of Colorado. Currently they're in Europe."

Damn, it would have been easier if they were home, more likely to scare off somebody loitering. Jade's other neighbor had a low picket fence. Nothing to give cover for their stalker. It was time to move.

"Remember, I say jump, you jump," he said, turning off the Rover's engine.

"Got it."

He ignored the slight quiver in her voice. "Then let's go. Stay to my right." He wanted to be between Jade and the tall fence.

They moved quickly to the porch, and he shielded her as she punched in the security code and the light turned green. She unlocked the door, and Malcolm pressed his hand on her back, pushing her through the door. Then he deadbolted the door behind them.

"Arm it. Please." He added the "please" after he noticed her drawn face and her arms wrapped around her middle as if she were holding her insides together.

She punched in the code and leaned against the door. "I thought I'd feel a sense of safety once I walked through the door. But instead, it feels just like a house, not a sanctuary."

Once again, he felt an uncomfortable emotional tug. He wanted to take a moment and make her feel better about her home. Wanted to gather her against him, hold her until she did feel safe.

All nonsense of course.

Jade jumped at the shrill tone of his phone ringing. It was Shelley from his office. He knew without looking as each of his major employees had their own ring tone.

"Hey, Boss. Got your texts."

"Shelley, got you on speakerphone." Jade was sidling away. He put a hand on her arm, wanting her to hear this conversation. "We're at Jade's house. Had a bit of trouble on the road. Did you clear my schedule?"

"Yep, and Mike is clear."

Malcolm paused, wondering if he was making the right decision assigning Jade to Mike.

"Boss?" Shelley questioned.

What the hell was he thinking? He didn't do this kind of work. Mike was the expert. They each had their own roles in the company, and he shouldn't cross the lines he'd set from day one.

See what happens when you crack that tough-guy veneer and let a little emotion in?

Malcolm released Jade's arm. "Still here. Get everyone over here ASAP."

"Okay. By the way, Megan called and is staying put at the

cabin as you requested, but she told me to tell you that fighting is better than hiding."

"Right. I'll call her in a bit." With that he punched off his phone and turned to face Jade. "Okay. You heard I've got a security team coming to work on your house. The system won't have a retinal scan, but it will have sensors and cameras."

"I'm okay with that."

He heard the unspoken "but" at the end of her sentence. Keeping his facial features bland, he simply waited for her to walk into his trap.

"I wasn't kidding when I said back at the morgue ... back in Denver, that it's vital I take part in finding Evan's killer. And who apparently killed my father as well. I will not sit here, wasting someone's time watching me twiddle my thumbs while I wait for answers."

Bingo. Trap sprung. Malcolm held up his hand, index finger extended. He forced away any emotion and spoke in what he hoped was a chilling, flat tone. "One, you have no experience in any of this." He lifted finger number two. "I don't have time to both actively protect you and be investigating." And now his final point, finger number three. "Because, in case you've forgotten, you have a target on your back. We, Megan and I," he emphasized Megan's name, "want you safe until this is over."

"But—"

"Jade, there is no but. I'll keep you in the loop. I'll need your input. But help in the field, no way." Folding his arms over his chest, he changed his stance, moving his feet apart, doing his best to look as serious as his words were.

"Megan said it best. Fighting is better than hiding. You need me," Jade said.

He knew she was going to be trouble—she was matching his tone, even his stance.

4

NEITHER SHE NOR MALCOLM MOVED AN INCH IN THE SMALL ENTRY hall of her house. Jade matched Malcolm's stare, willing him to understand that despite his two undeniable facts, the target on her back and her lack of investigative knowledge, she simply wouldn't hide in her house and be watched over.

Worse, to be told what she must do in such unyielding words and gestures was the wrong tactic to take with her. She had a stubborn streak, especially when she was sure she was correct.

Jade also knew full well her emotions were strung taut, yet his attitude rankled and smacked of what she'd often faced with her father, even Evan. Though never to this degree.

Her ire dissipated as quickly as it rose. What she wouldn't give for a little overprotecting from them now. But giving in wasn't her style either. And shedding more tears, at least right now, was useless and counterproductive.

She needed to find out who wanted her dead and why. At this moment, fighting Malcolm wasn't going to advance her case. She'd give in now and argue her point later. "Okay. Then what is our ... your first move?"

His cool gaze told her Malcolm wasn't the least bit fooled by her sudden capitulation. "The guys will be here shortly. But before they arrive, I'd like go over the events and figure out the timeline that preceded this."

Jade nodded. That made sense and would help focus her thoughts as well. "Do you mind if I change first? Then I can make some coffee since I need to be coherent and didn't drink much at your condo. Also, if you're hungry, there are some homemade muffins in the freezer," she offered, carefully keeping her words and voice neutral.

"I'll make the coffee, you go change. Do you want a muffin?"

"No, don't think I'm quite ready for food, but help yourself. I made orange cranberry and lemon poppy seed," she said over her shoulder as she left.

At the door to her bedroom she stopped, realizing this room that held her most personal and treasured objects felt as alien as the rest of her house. She headed into her en suite bathroom and splashed cold water on her face. Ignoring the mirror, she ran a comb through her short bob, then searched the closet for something casual to wear. Giving up quickly, she pulled on black leggings, a heavy fisherman-knit cream sweater that stopped mid thigh, and her favorite black ballet flats. All well-worn but giving her the only feeling of normalcy she'd had in the last twelve-plus hours.

Pulling back her shoulders, girding herself for what was coming, she headed back to the kitchen.

She noticed he'd not taken her up on her muffin suggestion. Was he like her, subsisting on caffeine to make it through moments of stress? Her stomach growled, but eating something wasn't possible at the moment. "Let me grab a cup and we can go into the living room."

"It's already done. I thought you could doctor it up to your liking." He handed her a mug decorated with multiple fleurs-delis, one she'd bought when she was a student at the Beaux-Arts de Paris.

How did he know? Regardless, his thoughtfulness disarmed her, and when she brushed past him to move into the living room, she felt his warmth and strength. For a nanosecond she wished she could just be enfolded in his arms and feel protected.

Shaking off those absurd longings, Jade quickly settled into her favorite reading spot, a large cream-colored club chair.

Malcolm surveyed the room and then picked the same place she'd stood only yesterday evening, in front of the fireplace, resting his elbow on the cherry mantle. Then he crossed his ankles, looking totally at ease.

She recognized that it was a good pose for an investigator. Nonthreatening. Interested, but keeping a professional distance. He looked ready.

She wasn't, but they had to move forward.

"Who knew the Kublai Khan was for sale?"

The question took a second to penetrate before Jade jumped to her feet. "Mrs. Cole. Oh my God. I can't believe I could forget something this important. She'll be furious, and I promised I'd send a car and didn't even get around to scheduling it. She'll know something is wrong. She had an inkling yesterday when Evan didn't show up on time. I've got to see her, explain that the Khan ... is missing. Tell her about Evan."

"You're not going out."

"I have to. Malcolm, you have weapons. You know what to watch for. This isn't something I can tell her over the phone."

She watched him think through all the angles. It was interesting to see his minute facial changes as he discarded each one.

He raised his gaze to meet hers. "We can go to her house."

"We?" He couldn't have shocked her more if he'd grown horns. "Why the sudden change of heart?"

"You need to talk to her. I need to observe Mrs. Cole's reactions."

Stunned by his about-face, she sank back into her chair.

"But not today. I know it's not good for business to ignore her, but you're not ready to see anyone. Can you put the office phone on voice messaging for the next few days, at least through the weekend?"

"I can't, but Megan can, even from home. Thankfully, she handles all that end of the business. And I think we can safely say today through Saturday. Sunday is always a no-business day."

Malcolm nodded. "Okay, I'll get her working on setting up the message when I see her later."

"You're going by Megan's?"

"Yeah, I'm going to check up on her. She was pretty shaken by Evan's death, and now that we're going to visit Mrs. Cole tomorrow, I'll stay there tonight. They have a crash room for me as I do for Greg at my condo. It'll be easier than driving back and forth from Denver."

While everything Malcolm suggested made sense, the thought of putting off a customer, even a difficult one like Mrs. Cole, went against the grain her father had instilled in her. But none of this was normal, and facing anyone and making any decisions right now seemed beyond her capabilities.

Jade fortified herself with a sip of the rich black coffee, drew a deep breath, and met his gaze squarely. "Back to the Kublai Khan. The sapphire recently came on the market, so anybody that followed high-end auctions or who was interested in gems would have known. Mrs. Cole has been a client of Laurent Art Brokers for years, at least while my father was alive. I hadn't heard from her since Dad died. She surprised me when she came to the office and asked me to be her agent for the auction.

"I found out only last week that other agents had turned her down."

"And they turned it down because of the curse?"

"How did you know about the curse?"

"Research last night. That's how I knew about your Beaux-Arts mug."

Yesterday seemed a million years long, and it shouldn't have surprised her that he had started working on the case, but it did. "People love curses as long as they aren't affected by them. Most dealers wouldn't worry about handling an object, as the owner would be the one affected by the curse." She shrugged, and looked into her coffee mug, wondering if what she said was true. "Or maybe nobody wanted a difficult client, and Mrs. Cole is that in spades."

"Do you believe in the curse?"

Jade fought the expected tremor. "I didn't." And she immediately wondered if Malcolm was a mind reader and had just read hers.

"Did anyone other than you and Megan know Evan's itinerary?"

"Just us three and of course the airlines."

"Does your office have any kind of encryption software?"

"We lock our computers at night. Back up anything important and put the flash drives into a small safe every night. But special software, no." It felt as if his questions were bullets coming at her. Bam. Bam. Bam. This needed to be done, she understood, and even admired his ability to keep his tone even and his expression neutral. However, she had no idea what he was thinking.

"And Evan. What kind of precautions did he take?"

Glancing down at her hands, she realized they were so

tightly clasped around the mug that they ached. She put the cup on the table next to her and rose, crossing the light wool rug to where Malcolm stood, and lifted a large silver frame from the mantle. "Here's my favorite picture of him." She touched the glass lightly before she held out the framed photo.

MALCOLM TOOK THE FRAME JADE HELD OUT TO HIM AND SCANNED the picture. Four men and Jade.

"Evan is on my left," she said softly. "Does that look like the man you saw at the morgue?"

Not at all. This Evan looked as if he were a scrapper, a more get-your-hands-dirty man, yet he bore just the slightest of smiles, as if he had a secret. The persona Malcolm had seen at the morgue was that of a man who wore wealth easily. "So he was a master of disguise. Why?"

Jade's eyes grew wide. "You know, I have no idea. I should, but I don't. He, Dad, and Omarr Basarias all worked together from before I was born until Dad decided he was bored with the gallery scene and opened Laurent Art Brokers in Boulder. It's funny, but I simply grew up with Evan being able to change appearances and personas like an actor. I never questioned it."

"Have you ever been threatened before?"

Malcolm noticed that Jade dropped her gaze and was nervously picking at her sweater, pausing before she answered. Something she hadn't done the entire time he threw questions at her. "What's bothering you?"

That had her finally lifting her head and meeting his gaze. "Dad seemed worried, especially the last two years. Which is why he put security in here, his house, and at the office. We don't keep artwork there, except of course for our owned work.

And I'll give you a little hint. It's all reproductions. The real work in is a vault in the Paris gallery."

Naturally Malcolm had heard about that kind of security but had never personally had clients who owned artwork valuable enough to keep in a vault. Expensive cars in a secure garage, maybe. "What do you think suddenly made him more safety conscious?"

"Dad was kind of old school. He didn't want me to worry, so he really told me nothing other than it was a good idea in general. I agreed to alarm, who wouldn't—"

She abruptly turned away, then as quickly turned back to him, her face pinched. "I wonder if I sent Evan to his death."

Malcolm jerked right out of his carefully orchestrated pose. "Why on earth would you think that?"

"He advised me against taking this commission, saying only that he had a bad feeling about it, nothing concrete. When I decided to act as broker, I also decided to be the courier. Evan absolutely refused to allow this. I tried to tell him that I could do it, but he assured me that he was better equipped. This last job would be his swan song—his words. I already told you he was retiring to Tuscany."

"So, you do believe?"

"No. Yes. I don't know. That's what I meant by saying 'I didn't' when you asked the first time. But he is gone, and he was carrying the Kublai Khan."

Her broken wail cut through his unemotional PI persona, and he wanted to gather her against him. But he pushed back his uncharacteristic response yet again.

Much like Evan, he wore a mask. Today it was his usual all-business face. When he was around clients, it's what they expected and wanted. But around family and his few friends such as Greg and Megan, he let that mask drop and was a softie. Proof? He was here because of Megan. Jade was her best friend.

Not entirely true, a little inner voice said. *There is something about Jade Laurent that interests you. And so does the case. A stolen, yet cursed gem. A dead courier and a woman who needs protection. Hollywood stuff.*

Pushing aside the emotional detour, he continued, back in his PI role. "Jade, I'm not much of a believer in curses. All we have right now is that Evan was murdered, didn't have the stone on his body ... person, yet it wasn't taken from him. And someone wants you dead."

Her hands trembled as she picked up the coffee cup, then put it back down.

He wasn't trying to be brutal but factual, and his attack right now was two-pronged. He needed information and she was in danger. She could help just by doing what she was doing now, *and* her safest place to be was here, behind secure doors. He didn't want any more nonsense about her being an active participant.

He studied the photo again. He recognized Gerard Laurent from the Internet search he'd made last night. In this picture he was dressed as what Malcolm imagined to be perfect character dress for a Parisian art dealer. Three-piece suit, dapper little mustache, one hand resting on the gold-wrought top of a walnut walking stick. His slight almond-shaped eyes were piercingly blue and held a hint of a deep sadness, in contrast to the smile gracing his mouth.

Jade must have gotten her auburn hair and incredible jade-green eyes from her mother. "Who are the other two men in the photo? They look like they're related."

She looked up from studying her coffee cup, though he'd bet she didn't see coffee but her imagined guilt.

"The man I mentioned earlier, Omarr Basarias, and his son Aksel."

Malcolm scanned the picture and realized Aksel was older

than Jade, then wondered why that surprised him. He was taller than the rest of the bunch, and the camera had captured his easy smile. In fact, as Malcolm studied the picture, he realized everyone smiled in some degree, yet their eyes told another story. "Tell me about Aksel."

"Aksel is ten years older than I. We all lived in Paris's 18th Arrondissement on the Rue des Saules within a stone's throw of each other. Aksel and Omarr lived above the gallery on the corner. Dad told me when he and Omarr were students at the École des Beaux-Arts they lived in that flat together. Dad moved out later when Omarr married. Aksel still lives there.

"Anyway, I was a nuisance to him, always following him around the gallery, or if he had friends around the Place du Tertre—"

"Which is?" Malcolm wondered if she realized how easily she slipped into her French accent.

"It's that famous painter's mecca, a square filled with artist's easels and sketch pads from early morning to late at night. I'm sure you've seen it in a gazillion movies. We lived very near the area. It was before my time, but Picasso used to walk around the square. Anyway, Aksel always had a great deal of patience with me. When Dad and I, along with Omarr, moved to Colorado, I was ten. Aksel was twenty and absolutely would not move to the States. He naturally went to Beaux-Arts and ran the gallery Dad and Omarr jointly owned. He is a true Parisian.

"When I was at school there, he was very busy with the business but always had time for me and for Evan, when he was there to teach."

"And where are Aksel and Omarr now? "

"Omarr died two years ago—"

"When?"

Thinking, Jade put down her mug. "Two years ago from

yesterday." Her voice held the realization that hit him before she got out the entire word.

"Your father died a year ago yesterday, and Evan ... yesterday. Too much coincidence. And I don't believe in coincidence," Malcolm stated in a deadly flat voice.

~

JADE STARED HARD AT HIM. HIS CERTAINTY ABOUT THE TWO deaths crumbled the remaining bedrock of stability her world had possessed. A madman was after the entire clan.

Clan. "Oh my God. Aksel is in danger as well!"

"Can you get him on the phone?"

Jade was already dialing the gallery in Paris. She didn't have another number for him. In fact, they hadn't been in touch since Omarr's death.

She put the phone in speaker mode. The message was in French, then English. "The gallery is currently closed. Please leave us a message and a clerk will return your call tomorrow."

Jade looked at Malcolm, mouthing "Should I leave a message?"

He nodded but held up his thumb and forefinger with a small space between them.

"Aksel, this is Jade. Call me right away, the moment you get this. And please," she hesitated, uncertain how much to say on a message, who might be listening to it before him. "Please be careful."

She disconnected.

"That was perfect. You couldn't really have said more because—"

"I know. All the while I wanted to scream at him to get away. But from what and whom?" She put the phone down and stared at the wool rug. Its woven patterns did nothing to ease any of the worry or the heartache. They had to find this madman before he could kill again.

"You said Evan lived in Boulder?"

It took a second for her to pull out of her chaotic thoughts. "Yes, why?"

"I'm guessing you have keys to his place?"

"Sure, I have a set. Again, why?"

"I want to see if there is anything in his files—"

She sat up straighter and met Malcolm's gaze directly. "Before Evan made this run for me, he made a point to remind me if anything ever happened to him, I should get a white envelope marked with my name out of his desk."

"You said earlier he was worried about something on this trip. Did you get the impression the envelope contains anything regarding his concern over this particular deal?"

"I don't think so. He started in on this envelope thing right after dad ... died."

"I'll get it for you tomorrow."

She knew she was going to push his buttons again. And maybe she was being a fool as he'd already agreed to one of her requests, to see Mrs. Cole. Nevertheless, finding the letter was vital. "Malcolm, you're not going alone—I'm coming with you."

"No."

"Yes. I. Am. I'll be with you."

"You're still safer here."

"Listen, I know his house. You'll be there, the doors will be locked, and you'll have your gun. It only makes sense."

He shook his head ever so slightly.

She pressed harder. She had to make him see it her way, this was too important. She didn't have a death wish, but neither could she just cave. "Malcolm, this point isn't negotiable. I can't hide."

Jade wasn't happy with his slight shrug but left the fight until later as she reeled in her chair, exhaustion and lack of food turning into light-headedness.

Just then Malcolm's phone beeped. He checked the text. "The guys are here. Listen, they don't need your help and can do your room first, then you can crash."

Crashing was exactly what her body needed. But not with them in the house. She didn't want them, she wanted the solid, if not always amenable, Malcolm by her side. Realizing as the thought caught her by surprise, that hadn't been alone since finding out about Evan.

"Let's get the door, I'll introduce you to the guys ..."

Jade got up to open the front door and immediately had to grab the chair's arms as the room tilted and spun.

"Sit, be still."

His words were sharp, but his tone was soothing, giving her a feeling of being cared for.

She sank back, accepting his words, grateful that he was here.

Malcolm let in his guys, then she heard rummaging in the kitchen. Moments later slices of ham, swiss cheese, and a sliced apple were set by her elbow.

"Eat. The guys will tell you when they're done with your bedroom, then you can get some sleep. I have a secure network, and they'll text me the code so I can let you know. Mike will be here shortly, and I'll be back in the morning so we can go to Mrs. Cole's house."

Jade wasn't excited about sleeping in the house as people worked. *But these people worked for Malcolm.* "Obviously, you trust your guys."

"With my life."

5

ON THE WAY TO THE CHAUTAUQUA CABIN THAT MEGAN SHARED
with Greg, Malcolm phoned Megan to warn her he was going to
crash there tonight and maybe longer. He was certain that
Megan would welcome his company and want to press him for
details on both Greg and Jade.

He had a few questions for her, as well as wanting her to set
up the phone message for Laurent Art Brokers. But mostly he
wanted to make sure she was okay after her visit to the morgue
and the revelation that Evan was not only murdered, but for
some reason lived a double life.

Malcolm yawned as he let himself into the cabin after
disarming the alarm. The first thing that hit him was the
tantalizing scent of chicken, chili powder, and onion.

"I was going to ask for an update, but later. Did you sleep at
all last night?" Megan called from the kitchen, then came into
the living room to give him a hug.

She held him extra tight, and he returned the hug as tightly.
Then she pushed him away so she could study him. "I would say
no sleep, and this case is turning into much more than you have
energy for."

"Geeze, thanks. I don't think I look that bad."

"Never, but I know you."

"Maybe a couple of hours of shut-eye in the last forty-eight," he admitted. "So I'm crashing, then I'll fill you in."

"I'm making chicken tortilla soup, and it'll be ready when you are."

"Perfect." He headed down the short hallway to the last room in the cabin. It was his whenever he needed it. The small room was paneled in warm yellow pine, complete with a bed, a closet that held several sets of clothes and blackout curtains so he could sleep no matter the time of the day.

One of the three bedrooms in his Denver condo was fitted out in similar fashion for Greg when he needed it.

Before he fell asleep standing up, he texted Shelley with the names of Omarr Basarias, his son Aksel, Evan Fischer, Gerard Laurent, and Mrs. Elvina Cole. He wanted his priceless assistant to do deeper research on all of them and mentioned that the info he'd been able to dig up was less than what he'd expected. He knew Shelley had friends in places Harrison & Talbot couldn't get access to, and if the information wasn't classified it would be shared.

It was midafternoon before he woke. Invigorated, he took a quick shower and changed into one of the sets of clothing he kept there. Refreshed, he headed into the cabin's living room.

Megan was curled up on the sofa, reading a book on Impressionist art. "I've got the soup simmering, and I turned on the coffee pot when I heard you taking a shower." She looked up from her book. "How is Jade?"

"Broken but strong. Stubborn and afraid. We had an incident on I-25 today, but while she was obviously scared spitless, she didn't fall apart," Malcolm said as he grabbed a cup from the ancient pine cupboards and filled it with the brew. There was no doubt he was a coffee addict. One thing he had in common with Jade. He quickly dismissed even that minor connection, as he felt he'd already stepped across the boundary between client and PI.

Megan scooted over on the couch and patted the spot where she'd made room for him to sit. "I've told you countless times, she's as tough as I am. Do you think for a minute that I love it when Greg goes undercover and can't communicate, like now? Or the two of you are on a stakeout? No, I hate it, but I deal with it."

She took the mug out of his hands and put it on the table. He knew she had another important point to make.

"I have three people in my life that I cherish. Greg, you, and Jade. And at this moment, two of them are in danger. Find this insane person and fix this."

"Yes, ma'am." He felt a soft punch to his arm, then was handed back his mug.

"Do you want food or your computer first?"

"Actually, food." He was hungry but could have waited to eat. However, he knew Megan was hungrier for information about Greg. That conversation over dinner and wine last night hadn't happened. So now, over this meal, would be the perfect time to bring her up to date.

MALCOLM PUT HIS SPOON DOWN AFTER INHALING HALF OF HIS bowl of soup. He patted his stomach. "Greg told me he misses your cooking."

"Is that all he misses?" Megan wiggled her eyebrows.

Despite her attempt at lightness, Malcolm heard the longing in her voice. He knew Greg was in the field too much and planned on a conversation with him about this soon. "I'm sure not. He'll be home in about a week."

"That's good news. I know you can't say anything more about him."

Yep, definitely that conversation had to be had with Greg. He loved field work, but Malcolm knew it was wearing on him as well. Time to change the subject as he'd said everything he could about Greg. "Meg, did you ever meet Omarr Basarias?"

She looked up from buttering a hot tortilla. "A couple of times. He seemed like he was carrying a burden. He'd smile and was as gracious as Gerard, but there always seemed to be a shadow, or a maybe he carried a secret."

"What about his son, Aksel?"

"Nope, never met him. Just know that he and Jade were close. I don't suppose you're going to tell me why you're asking me and not Jade."

"I did ask her, but Jade is too close to them and the deaths to see anything but memories. And—" He paused, then decided it was important to let Megan know why she was going to remain under house arrest. He put his spoon down.

Megan followed his action, then waited.

"Omarr died two years ago to the day of Gerard's hit and run. Evan exactly a year from Gerard's death."

"You mean they're related and the note left for Jade meant she's next now, not in a year. The clock ticking down meant *now*?"

Malcolm simply nodded.

"Oh my God on so many levels." She slapped a hand to her mouth. "Mrs. Cole, has Jade contacted her?"

"We're heading over tomorrow morning to break the news."

"Should I come?"

"No. Here is exactly where you should be."

"But who will man the office? I have to handle the clients once news gets out, and you know it will."

"You can't go to the office until this is over, Meg."

She looked at him steadily. "You mean not until you've caught this bastard and it's over, right? Not that it's over because ..."

"Right. Jade would like you to put a message on the office phone system that Laurent Art Brokers is closed until Monday."

Megan nodded and got up, cleared the table, and replenished his coffee. Then she put together a container of soup and tortillas for him to take to Jade tomorrow morning.

Pretty soon, he bet she'd start baking, something she did when Greg was on a case. Now both her fiancé and her best buddy were in harm's way.

He knew better than to offer any help—she needed activity, and this was all she could do at the moment. Energized with food and Megan's soft, uncomplicated presence, he opened the computer stashed in its own "safe room" just like the one he had at his condo. Waiting for the information he'd requested from Shelley, he finished the files on his last case and sent them off.

The computer chimed and he glanced at the screen.

Boss, not much more info on Fischer, Laurent, or Basarias senior. In fact, what is there is so superficial it means something. I'm getting Jana involved. It's the FBI's modus operandi of what information they want to release. You can always tell. Mrs. Elvina Cole's information, on the other hand, wasn't buried. I'm attaching the basics.

Evan Fischer. Age 66. Born in Iowa. Five foot six, brown hair and eyes. Lost right arm in a tractor accident. Scholarship to the University of Colorado. Graduated in Art History. Never married.

Gerard Laurent, Jade's father. The only son of art professors at Les École des Beaux-Arts. Never married. Taught at the same school.

That was odd. Who was Jade's mom? He read on.

Omarr Basarias, Aksel's father. Taught at same school. Son of art professors at same school.

Mrs. Elvina Cole, née Keller. Age 70. Moved to United States with husband in the 70s. Expensive public schools in England. Husband

deceased, Elvina sole beneficiary. Relatives now deceased, but were
high up in the British armed forces. Son David Cole, age 40. Founder
of a high-tech company, Blue Wave, that is worth billions.

Shelley was right. There was definitely not enough
information to go on for the trio of men. And where did Mrs.
Cole get her money to buy the Khan? From her son?

Pushing the computer back into its hidden cubby, Malcolm
paced the living room. The early spring sun was setting. He
needed a run or a hike.

Suddenly he understood both Jade's and Megan's need to be
out, to do something.

He hadn't been told what to do since law school and their
no-job policy. Even then he could hit the trails or do whatever
was needed to release tension.

Unsettled by these revelations and hyped up with caffeine
and frustration, he returned to his tiny room and laced his
hiking boots, then shrugged on a down vest. "Meg, I'm going to
hike the loop."

She stepped out of the kitchen, a large glass mixing bowl
cradled in her arm. "Dinner or cookies when you get back?" She
nodded toward the bowl. "This is my fifth batch in the last ten
days. The freezer is full."

"Worry-baking again?"

She lifted her shoulders in a shrug, and Malcolm made an
instant mental note not to send anyone married or with a
significant other on undercover or stakeout assignments from
now on. There were plenty of good, unattached men and
women who could do the job as well as Greg or himself.

You? You are unattached. You can still do all this, his inner voice
said.

But I don't want to.

Pushing away the unaccustomed self-revelation, he
answered Megan's question. "How about a salad, glass or two of

wine, and cookies for dessert. Since your freezer is bulging, I'll take some to Jade's tomorrow as well as the soup. Mike loves your cookies."

"Jade loves them too. She snags a bunch and eats them when no one is looking."

Funny, he truly could see this. Jade seemed to be about appearances, and that may have been Gerard's influence. But he could see her indulging in something nearly sinful, like Megan's cookies or ...

Clearing his throat, he made a point of checking that he had his phone. Totally unnecessary, but hopefully the movement covered his wanton thoughts.

Not. Megan wore a lopsided grin.

Making sure the cabin's alarm was on after he closed the door behind him, he tackled the hike, moving faster than normal, even in the waning light.

The route took him up a steep hill, and as it was now very late afternoon, the sun had dropped behind the massive Flatirons and the air was brisk and crisp.

Perfect for clearing his mind. Yet it wouldn't clear. Images of the past two days played in a loop. He needed clarity, yet he could see only the past.

His phone chirped. It was the head of his security installation team. "Talbot."

"We're done."

"You're ahead of schedule."

"Well, Ms. Laurent looked like she was asleep on her feet. She wouldn't use her bedroom, even though we worked on it first. So we hustled. I'm sending the codes now. Mike is here, and they met. Seemed to hit it off, even though Ms. Laurent was pretty adamant that with the additional security, she was safe without him. I'm sure she'll head to her room the moment we're gone."

"Thanks." There was nothing more to be said, but he'd make sure a bonus was tucked into their paychecks. His team wasn't on call, and this job pulled them away from their families.

Feeling better now that Jade's house was properly protected, he took a turn from McClintock trail onto Enchanted Mesa, past the reservoir and headed down to Megan's cabin. She and Greg were getting married in July, followed by a thirty-day honeymoon. Malcolm would miss his partner and he was sure Jade would miss Megan for the duration, but it was Megan's first time out of the country and Greg didn't want to rush the trip.

"And life will be back to normal, and the bastard out to kill Jade behind bars," he said to nothing but the scrub brush, pine trees, and a squirrel that looked up inquiringly.

6

JADE DRESSED CAREFULLY FOR THE DIFFICULT DAY AHEAD, PICKING a pencil-skirted suit in a deep rust. Donning brown tights and her three-inch suede heels, she then brushed on a coat of mascara and a swipe of color to her lips but otherwise didn't worry about her wan complexion.

She was ready for battle.

Liar.

Okay, she'd never be ready. But telling Mrs. Cole that her precious Khan was missing and Evan dead, all the while trying to keep the woman's fury below DEFCON 1 was going to take every bit of skill Jade possessed.

Meaning she had to push her own grief and fear to the background.

She walked into the kitchen to find her bodyguard, Mike, sitting at the counter. He stood immediately, as if he were in the military and she the general. Maybe she should salute.

"Sit. Would you like a cup of coffee? You can always help yourself, any time."

"No, ma'am."

"Jade," she corrected yet again, after at least a dozen times yesterday afternoon. Mike even had the closely cropped hair of the military, so that it looked almost like a dark stain over his head.

"Yes, ma'am. I brought everything I need, so I'll be fine."

His grin made him human, as did the quickly masked twinkle in his brown eyes. She hadn't seen it yesterday as he'd surveyed the yard and her home while the "security team" was installing the new alarm system or while they'd been talking. She was sure it was the nicest interrogation she'd ever been a part of. Far nicer than Malcolm's staccato questioning.

Even so, as exhausted as she was yesterday, it had taken her a long time to fall asleep with a stranger in the house.

She nuked a muffin, then picked at it as she waited for Malcolm, her stomach protesting even the few morsels that passed her lips. She knew she needed to eat but couldn't manage it.

He arrived at 9 o'clock on the dot, dressed in dark slacks, a collarless shirt, and a tweed sports jacket, carrying a brown paper grocery-type bag with handles. "From Megan."

She opened the bag and sniffed. "Soup and cookies?"

He nodded.

She put away the food, telling Mike about the cookies and getting another grin. Then she returned to Malcolm and braved his once-over.

"Is that your business attire?" he asked with a raised brow and slight smile.

"Usually not this severe, but yes, I wear suits when I meet with specific clients. What about you?"

"This is as dressy as I get. Though apparently Megan is having the guys wear tuxes at the wedding." He grimaced. "I've only worn a penguin suit once, and it was like wearing a costume."

"Megan promised me no frou-frou gowns, but we have yet to

go shopping." Their conversation was normal, and she realized they were both trying to create a façade behind which she'd fight to control this meeting with Mrs. Cole.

"Honestly," he pointed to himself, "what I'm trying for with the clothes is to make a good enough impression that your Mrs. Cole will ignore me, and I can watch her without her watching me. From the bio I've read about her, she seems very into appearances. And I want my presence there to be nearly invisible."

"You've nailed her. This is going to be a difficult conversation. She doesn't like me, but she loved my father, who made sure she was handled with kid gloves. I can't live up to his service level. Another sticking point is that her son, David, who is the shining light in her life, and I date occasionally when he's in town. That gets her dander up."

Jade only realized she was looking for Malcolm's reaction at her mention of dating David after he didn't do anything. His face remained totally bland.

That too is a reaction, silly. And why do you care?

"I read up a bit on David Cole as well. He's done extremely well with his software company."

"Yeah. He's up in the billionaire category. But he's a really nice guy who is very kind and generous to his mother. Even if he lives about as far away from her as one can and still live in the States."

"That bad, huh? Okay, then. Are you ready?"

She shrugged but nodded.

"Remember, if either Mike or I give a command, do it."

Malcolm and Mike didn't move until she nodded again. As if her acceptance was a signal, they marched her out the door and locked up. Sandwiched between them, Jade reached the Range Rover.

Malcolm waited to drive off until Mike returned to the

house and the door shut behind him. Mike's presence still seemed excessive, yet she acknowledged a bit more calmness because she had the best of the best, Harrison & Talbot, on her side.

"HERE'S THE ADDRESS." MALCOLM DROVE PAST THE HOUSE AND stopped, then backed into Mrs. Cole's long stone paved driveway.

Jade turned in her seat, noticing that the driveway curved past the rear of the house, very much a mansion style. No garage would dare show its face.

Then she took in the house, a stunning Tudor, and so very English.

Mrs. Cole's home boasted a dramatic peaked and shingled roof. The exterior was a combination of brick, chiseled stone, and decorative half-timbering. Many sets of tall narrow windows in the second story were set with tiny windowpanes, and a large bow window front and center of the ground floor featured the same small, glittering panes.

The architecture was remarkable, as would the landscaping be once spring finally sprung. A perfectly manicured lawn with hedgerows edging the garden and lining the stone steps up to a heavy wooden door on the left side of the mansion and urns flanking each side of the door. Jade could picture them overflowing with flowers and greenery.

"Okay, same routine. I say move, you do it."

Her momentary bubble of peace popped, and she glared at him. "I think it's time for you to drop the commando language. I will do my best to do exactly what you say. You've reminded me every time. I've. Got. It."

Malcolm turned in his seat to face her. Sunglasses hid his

eyes, but his tightened lips said it all. "This isn't a game, Jade. This is about keeping you alive."

Fighting to control the automatic shudder that coursed through her, Jade summoned up a bit of her tenacious grit. "I understand, but I won't cower either. And I will not be intimidated by you and this ... this macho attitude you turn on and off at will. This is my life and the business my father and his friends built up over the years. I have their reputation to uphold, let alone my own. Today might well be the beginning of the end of it once Mrs. Cole finds out about her damned stone."

Jade realized she was yelling. Turning away from his gaze, she stared straight ahead, out the front window of the Range Rover, not daring to look at Malcolm's reaction to her outburst. She knew the day was going to be difficult if not impossible, but it had started off with a reasonable tone. Now she felt brittle, like a windshield that had a pit in it and was about to shatter in a zigzag across her life.

She wanted to apologize, yet she meant every word she'd said. Instead she clasped her hands tightly in her lap and fought for the calm she'd need to face Mrs. Cole by taking one deep shuddering breath after another.

Warmth covered her hands and she glanced down to see Malcolm rubbing his thumb over her whitened knuckles. His gesture startled her as much as it warmed her.

Taking a chance, she looked over to see that he'd pushed his sunglasses up on his head. His gaze held understanding, not anger.

"Okay. Got your message. I won't bark at you as long as you understand—"

"I understand it all—" Jade held up her hand.

"Let's get through this." Malcolm copied her gesture. "I'm sorry I added to your stress. Before we go confront the lion, I have a question."

Jade blinked, surprised that he had the guts to apologize. "Shoot." Then she slapped a hand to her mouth. "Bad choice of words. Ask away."

His slight smile brought them back to the mood of this morning.

"Did Mrs. Cole insure the Khan?"

"Of course. For the full $7 million."

"Was it difficult for her to get the insurance? Did she mention any problems to you?"

"No. In fact, it all happened very quickly. Why?"

"I wanted to see if anything sounded out of the norm. To figure out if there was any reason for Mrs. Cole to have planned this robbery."

Jade thought about his statement, then shook her head. "Though she desperately wanted the stone, I can't see her stealing something she technically already owned. Mrs. C has plenty of money, though I think most of it comes from David." She thought for a minute more. "Furthermore, wouldn't she be the first person the authorities would question? Why risk getting caught?"

"Wait, back up. You said, 'desperately wanted.' Why do you say that?"

"There isn't much factual history behind the story of the sapphire." Jade twisted in her seat to face him fully. "When the Ottoman forces were defeated in Europe by Russia, England objected to the treaty of San Stefano between Russia and Turkey, stating it gave Russia too much power and territory. That is fact.

"This next part is according to Mrs. Cole—it's not written down anywhere. The Kublai Khan was given to Mrs. Cole's great grandfather by Queen Victoria for his part in the negotiation of the Treaty of Berlin in 1878, which reversed some of the territory claimed by Russia."

"Valuable token," Malcolm commented. "Is there more?"

"Yes, and this is fact as well. Colonel Keller, Mrs. Cole's great grandfather, started researching the gem's so-called curse after a string of family incidents began happening. Among other things, one of his daughters was killed when she fell off a horse taking a jump. And his son unexpectedly lost a fortune on business deals."

"Why would Mrs. Cole want anything to do with a jinxed stone?"

"Historically, I think anything valuable that has a superstition attached gives the owner cachet. Did you know the Hope diamond is supposed to be jinxed?" Jade shrugged. "Anyway, Mrs. C stated emphatically that she didn't believe in curses or spells. That the stone belonged in her family, period."

"So then Mrs. Cole had already paid you for the gem?"

"Actually, she had a letter of credit that I used in the auction. I was a phone bidder. But yes, the Khan is hers."

"Then you're right, none of this makes any sense. She wouldn't steal a stone she's already paid for. As you said, money is no object for her."

"True." Jade grabbed his arm in excitement. "But remember, she also insured the gem. What if she could get the insurance money *and* have the stone, therefore not having to pay for it, since she already believes the Khan belongs to her family?"

"That's a very good thought."

A wave of warmth flowed through her at his unexpected praise.

"So how did this sapphire come to be called the Kublai Khan?"

"Legend has it that Genghis Khan gave each of his sons a gem that would bring them strength. There were shrines created for each gem. The four sons, now fathers, passed the gem's power to the son they thought would be the strongest. Kublai conquered most of China. At some point his gem was stolen. And the curse was born."

"Wow, that is some history, true or not."

"One other bit of info before we see Mrs. Cole. She admitted that the Colonel was forced to sell the gem because of his son's debts. Shortly after, Colonel Keller died."

"So really it's possible this stone was stolen heritage. That could cause all sorts of issues, even murder, to get it back," Malcolm said.

"I guess I didn't think of it that way, but yes. Though the last few owners had documentation that it was theirs legally. Thus, the sales could be legitimate."

"Very convoluted. As I said, I'll be watching her very closely. Unless she's a very good actress, she'll be shocked on both counts. The missing stone and Evan's death."

As if he knew his words would hurt, he covered her hands again. Jade deeply appreciated his supportive touch and his awareness of the pain his mention of Evan caused.

"Ready?" he asked. "I'll be with you all the way."

Leaving the Rover, she stayed close to Malcolm, realizing as she did so that he hadn't barked commands at her.

As they approached the door, it was flung open. "Finally. You should have called, I've been frantic. Come in, come in."

THEY ENTERED THE ELEGANT FOYER AND FRANKLY, IT WOULDN'T have surprised Malcolm if a butler in a wig popped into the room to speak with "madame" or "your majesty," as Mrs. Cole's proper British accent sounded noble.

Malcolm brought up the rear as Jade followed Mrs. Cole. They passed through to a dark, wood-paneled living room filled with furniture that looked as if it was from a castle in England.

Tapestries hung on two walls, providing a majestic background for the woman before him. She even looked and dressed similarly to the Queen herself. Neatly styled white hair, full tweed suit, enormous pearls at her neck. But the perfume! He stifled a sneeze.

The lady of the house didn't offer them a seat. Obviously, Mrs. Cole was very put out. Jade knew it as well as she squared her shoulders and breathed in deeply.

"Mrs. Cole, this is Malcolm Talbot—"

"Of Harrison and Talbot Investigations," Malcolm continued smoothly as he extended his hand in greeting, not surprised that she extended her hand, slightly touching his.

She scrutinized him, then nodded to herself. "Harrison and Talbot. I've heard of you. Why are you here with Jade? And where is my precious Khan?"

The last sentence was directed at Jade, and he kept close watch on Mrs. Cole as Jade moved forward to face her directly.

"Mrs. Cole, Evan is ... Evan is dead, and the sapphire is missing. Mr. Talbot is working—"

The older woman thrust up a hand as if warding off the flow of Jade's words. "Stolen? Murdered? No. Impossible. David wouldn't, couldn't have ..." She turned ashen under her layers of makeup, pressing one hand against her chest as she crumpled.

Malcolm caught her and carried her to the sofa.

"Pills ... in the drawer ... of the side table ... small white ones." She struggled to speak.

"Jade, get a glass of water, then call 911," Malcolm ordered as he stretched the thin woman out on the couch and checked for her pulse, concerned to find it so faint.

Jade returned with the water and was dialing 911.

Quickly finding the vial of pills, he poured one into his palm. "Open your mouth."

Popping in a pill, he held the cup of water to her lips.

She brushed his hand away. "Under tongue, nitro ..."

"Glycerin?" Malcolm finished for her.

She nodded weakly, then struggled to speak again.

"You can tell me later." He searched her face, hoping to see some color return.

Jade sat on the arm of the sofa, holding her hand. Even though Mrs. Cole obviously didn't approve of Jade, that didn't stop her from offering what comfort she could to the stricken woman.

Malcolm met Jade's gaze, seeing fear and confusion. He nodded slightly. He didn't understand why Mrs. Cole mentioned her son either.

Minutes passed and finally Malcolm heard sirens heralding the arrival of the paramedics.

The cavernous living room soon bustled with people in action. Malcolm handed one EMT the vial of pills as the others stabilized the elderly lady and readied her for transport. "We'll take her to Boulder Community Health. Any relatives?"

Mrs. Cole strained to speak through the oxygen mask. "David. Jade, call him."

"I will," Jade assured her.

The ailing woman, now wrapped in a blanket and strapped to the gurney, blinked once, then closed her eyes. The paramedics hustled the stretcher out to the ambulance. Jade was about to follow, but Malcolm put a hand on her arm and closed the door behind the paramedics, so he and Jade remained in the house. "I thought it might be better to call him from here. I want to listen carefully, so—"

"Speaker, got it."

Malcolm nodded, privately pleased that Jade didn't fight him and understood what he was trying to do. Like a partner.

Why did that pop into his head? Then he realized it was

because she kept repeating that she wanted to be a part of this. That she *must* help.

Jade held up the phone as they waited for David to answer.

"Cole, here."

"David? Jade. I'm at your mother's house. She was just taken to the hospital, a cardiac issue. Are you in Hawaii?"

"No, I've been in Denver for a meeting and was about to return home. The plane is loading. God, what caused it?"

"The Khan—"

Malcolm touched her arm, and put a finger to his lips, telling her he didn't want her to say anything more. Thankfully, she nodded her understanding.

"She wants you."

"Of course, I'll be there as quickly as possible. Which hospital?"

Jade told him and signed off.

Malcolm shook his head. "He sounded completely shocked. I don't believe that was faked. Maybe we'll get a chance to ask him more questions in person. You two are close, right?"

"Good friends."

Malcolm quirked his brow, wanting to know a bit more. "Friends? You dated, right?"

Jade leaned against the door. He didn't want to probe into her life, but she and David were connected. Mrs. Cole seemed to think her son had done something, so Malcolm needed to dig deeper.

"Right," she said with a sigh. "A couple of kisses, lots of talk about life. He's a nice guy, geeky, too involved with his software business. I know he wasn't keen on his mother purchasing the stone, but she was adamant that it was part of the Keller/Cole dynasty, that it belonged with her. I also think, as I said, he most likely put up the money for her to buy it."

"Yet her worry about her son potentially being involved

caused her heart issue. So right now everyone is a suspect. Everyone."

Jade's shoulders slumped and she looked at the floor. "I can't see it. It doesn't feel right."

Malcolm gently placed a finger under her chin, raising it so she'd have to look at him. "You never know what's hiding inside a person. I've found some of the most mild-mannered, good-looking people can hide twisted minds. Look at any number of murderers—Ted Bundy, for example. One mother said he appeared to be the very type of young man she'd like her daughter to go out with. Lesson number one, don't make prejudgments, especially with people you know.

Ignoring her questioning look, he opened Mrs. Cole's door and scanned the area. Quiet, no new cars parked on the block. "Just remember, right now everyone is a suspect. Everyone."

He twisted the door handle lock button, glanced at her, and got her nod. Closing the door behind them, he quickly checked to make sure it locked, then they hustled toward the Range Rover.

7

BEFORE THEY REACHED THE ROVER, MALCOLM'S PHONE RANG IN the distinctive tone that meant urgent. Crap. "Talbot."

"Mike. Got an issue. My nephew didn't come home, but his baseball did with a cryptic note rubber-banded around it. *Standing Guard Means Losing One.* Sorry, Boss, but I'm heading to my sister's. Jade's house is locked and armed."

"Move," Malcolm said to Jade, at the same time pocketing the phone and hitting the unlock button on the SUV. "Back seat, my side, don't go around."

She moved fast and practically dove into the car.

"Stay down."

"Got it."

Malcolm squealed out of the driveway and sped down Linden Drive to Broadway. He hit the phone button, calling Mike back.

"I've got Jade. Keep me informed. Put your family into one of the safe houses. Or my condo if you feel it's necessary."

"Thanks." And the line went dead.

"What was that all about?" Jade's voice trembled.

"Somebody took Mike's nephew. He's gone to help."

Malcolm squealed to a stop, just missing the green light. "Sorry, you okay back there?"

"Yeah. You think it has something to do with me?"

"I don't know. Mike has worked a lot of cases, but then why now for retaliation?"

"Yeah."

A few more slow minutes passed, keeping Malcolm at high alert. Finally, they were in her neighborhood. "Okay, we're turning onto your street. I'm going to cruise by your house, turn around, and come back if it looks okay. Then we'll hustle inside —damn!"

"What?"

"Stay down for now. There is an unfamiliar car parked in front of your house and a guy sitting on your front steps. He seems totally at ease, but we can't be too careful now that Mike has apparently been lured away.

"When I tell you to look, rise up enough just to see if you recognize him. It'll be hard for him to see into the darkened back windows, so I think the odds of him recognizing you are pretty slim."

Malcolm drove closer and slowed down a bit. "Now."

He kept his eyes on the road before them, wondering if this guy was a decoy to distract them. He felt for his 9mm nestled between the console and his seat, pulled it out, and placed it on his lap.

He'd nearly passed her house and wasn't getting a good feeling about this as Jade hadn't yet answered.

"Malcolm, it's Aksel."

"Are you sure. Why did you hesitate?"

"I haven't seen him in a couple of years. Then he had a long ponytail and a beard. Now it's that fashionable day-old beard look and close-cropped hair. But nothing can hide that mouth or that chin. I know it's Aksel even if he's wearing sunglasses."

Malcolm glanced at her in the rearview mirror. The lightness in her voice and the curve of her lips touched a nerve. Aksel made her smile. He made her worry.

"It's cold out. Why isn't he waiting in the car?"

Jade's smiled dimmed. "I have no idea, but it's Aksel. Malcolm, I want to, I *need* to see him. And recall, you thought he could be a target too, your words. We need to warn him."

As there wasn't room to park behind Basarias's car on the street, Malcolm pulled into Jade's cobbled driveway. He didn't like it that he could be blocked from the rear, but they weren't going to be here long. He put the 9mm into his waist holster and patted it. Perhaps from habit or maybe for luck. "Together, okay?"

"Okay."

Malcolm heard the excitement dim in her voice and hated it.

Walking side by side up the driveway, they approached her friend, who watched them with an easy smile lifting his lips. The sunglasses were still on, so there was no way for Malcolm to gauge his eyes.

Aksel stood and moved down the steps when they were within five feet. He opened his arms. "Jade, *ma chérie*! I got your cryptic message."

She walked into her friend's embrace, hugging him tightly. Then he took a step back, cupped her face, and kissed her on both cheeks.

Aksel's accent rubbed Malcolm the wrong way. It felt affected. But it didn't seem to bother Jade at all. And after all, the man lived in Paris. Maybe it was their easy friendship that bothered Malcolm.

He noted her childhood friend was nearly as tall as his own six-plus feet. Dressed in a pewter-colored parka from an expensive maker, a black sweater showing at the neckline, and black jeans, he looked like a fashion model, but with the lean, taut look of an athlete.

"*Merci, mon cher ami*," Jade replied. "When did you get into town? How did you find me?"

"Evan, of course. I contacted him about a week ago when I decided it was time to visit you both. I've missed you, *chérie,* and though I've been here a few days, I thought maybe we could visit him together before he leaves for Italy." He raised his arms, palms up. "Why was your message so cryptic? Be careful? Of what?"

"I think we should go inside," Malcolm said in a voice he hoped would brook no resistance.

Aksel cocked his head slightly. "Who is this?" he asked Jade.

"We can do the introductions inside, okay?" Malcolm pushed Jade in front of him, so she mounted the stairs first. Before he could disarm the house alarm, a car pulled up behind Malcolm's Rover, and he immediately reached for his holstered gun.

He relaxed a bit when he saw Tomba and Moore emerge from the unmarked, dark sedan.

"Hold up, Talbot, Ms. Laurent."

"Can we do this inside?" Malcolm made it a question but gave them a look that allowed none other than an affirmative answer.

"Sure, no problem."

JADE STOOD TO THE SIDE AS MALCOLM DISARMED THE DOOR, using a code on his phone, and guided her inside with a hand on her back. His action felt protective, not pushy. And she hoped the two Denver homicide detectives' unexpected presence meant good news for her. Maybe Malcolm would be unnecessary in the future.

Oddly, that was a disappointing thought.

As glad as she was to see Aksel and resume an active friendship with him, their lives had taken different paths. Jade wasn't looking for a boyfriend or a lover, but a male friend. Something like Megan had with Malcolm would be a welcome addition to her life once it was back to a semblance of normal.

And hopefully she'd hear just that from either Tomba or Moore in the next few minutes.

Jade led everyone the few feet into the living room. Nobody bothered to sit. Including herself. This wasn't a social call, after all.

"I hope you're bringing me good news." Jade addressed the skinny one, trying to remember if he was Tomba or Moore.

The heavier detective opened his mouth. Now she remembered—he was Tomba.

"Were you aware that Evan Fischer had a will, Ms. Laurent?" Tomba spoke in his official voice.

"Will?" Aksel parroted.

"No. I had no idea." She turned to her friend, uncertain how to deliver the tragic news. "Evan was murdered two days ago." She softened her voice, trying to lessen the blow.

"Impossible. We emailed just a week ago. He was happy about Tuscany."

The disbelief in Aksel's voice pushed Jade to move closer to her old buddy, to share their loss with an embrace. Instead, he moved back a step, stopping Jade in her tracks. His reaction confused and hurt her. Sure, they'd not lived near each other for over a decade, but they had a history. A long, family-like history, and now only the two of them were left.

"Aksel, it's just us now—"

"Ms. Laurent," Tomba interrupted. "You are the beneficiary

of said will. To the tune of at least a million. Plus all the assets he owned."

"What the hell are you inferring?" Malcolm bristled at the implication.

"It's obvious what I mean. At the moment Jade is the prime suspect in Fischer's death. Follow the money."

Nausea welled up in her throat. Fleeing the room, she hoped she'd make it to the bathroom.

Not taking the time to turn on the light, she slammed the door shut. What little food she'd had the past few days turned into dry heaves. Finally sitting against the wall of the small room, she gathered her tattered emotions.

"Jade?" Malcolm called through the closed door.

"I'm fine. I'll be out in a minute. Have they gone?"

"No. But I'm going to ask them to leave. All of this can be done tomorrow."

"Ask Aksel to stay. We need to talk to him."

She didn't want to get up. Huddling on the bathroom floor in the dark was preferable to just about anything else she had to face. And while her father more often than not had metaphorically cocooned her in bubble wrap to avoid some of the harsher realities of life, this wasn't something that could be avoided.

Getting to her knees, then her feet, she felt for the light and flipped the switch.

Then let loose a scream that tore her throat.

HER SCREAM CHILLED MALCOLM TO THE BONE. SPRINTING BACK the short distance, he wrenched open the door and found her slumped on the floor against the vanity. No blood, no obvious wounds.

His instant relief was milliseconds long as he read the words scrawled in bold black marker on the mirror.

I WAS WRONG, TWO MORE TO GO. AND YOU'RE FIRST.

"Malcolm, please take me out of here," Jade moaned.

He lifted her gently into his arms, and the three other men backed out and away as he carried her into the living room and laid her on the couch. Aksel followed closely and when Malcolm released Jade, sat next to her.

"We'll check outside, take a look at the security system." Tomba led the way to the door with Moore right behind him.

Malcolm nodded and turned back to Jade.

Pale, deathly still, with eyes still closed, she looked like a porcelain doll.

Malcolm was grateful she had somebody she loved by her side right now. He needed to think. Too many things were going south with this case. Mike had been called away, with no longer than fifteen minutes passing between that phone call and Malcolm getting to Jade's house.

"How long were you sitting on the steps before we arrived?" he asked her friend quietly.

"No more than five minutes."

Whoever was after Jade had killed Evan and probably both Jade's and Aksel's fathers, and that person was one step ahead of them now. Malcolm pulled out his cell phone and moved to the kitchen. Quickly, he completed the arrangements and waited for his firm's computer system to encrypt the call.

Aksel came in, grabbed a glass of water and a folded tea towel lying on the counter, ran it under water, and wrung it out. "For Jade."

Malcolm nodded and just as Aksel left, his call was picked

up. Everything would be ready in less than an hour and there was a bonus to boot. He pocketed his phone and headed into the living room.

Aksel sat on the ottoman next to the couch.

"Why did you back away from me?" Jade asked after taking a sip of water.

"*Chérie*, it wasn't you. It was the horror of the words I was hearing. Evan, dead, murdered. I'd wanted to regain that friendship, and now it is too late."

"Basarias," Malcolm interrupted. "We need to get you somewhere safe. Jade and I uncovered a connection that means you could well be the second person the scrawl on the mirror alluded to."

If possible, Jade paled even more. Malcolm hated this, but it was time to be blunt.

"What connection?"

Basarias blanched as well. Not surprising, as he'd just been marked for death.

"Your father, Gerard, and Evan were all killed one year apart, but the note—"

"What note?"

Jade leaned forward and reached for Aksel's hand. He grasped it and held it tight. "There was a note next to Evan's body that very politely told me I was next. And we don't think this is going to be a year from Evan's ... death."

"And what, there will be a note for me on your death?"

"Well, that's not the plan, naturally—"

Malcolm interrupted. "If this nut job can't get to Jade, then he may change the order. Have you received any odd phone calls, letters, texts—"

"Yes. I did get a strange text about Basarias et Fils and the sins of the father."

"Basarias et Fils?"

"Our galleries' name. There is one in Paris and one in Denver."

"Omarr ran the Denver gallery and Aksel the original gallery in Paris. The one I told you about," Jade clarified.

"I'm actually thinking of selling the Denver Gallery and only having Paris.

"What?"

"*Chérie*, Paris is my blood. The city speaks to me. I'm happy with my small gallery on Rue des Saules. Art, wine, and bread, and I'm happy."

"That is hogwash, but it's a good line for a movie," Jade said.

"Do you come to Denver often?" Malcolm asked.

Aksel had the grace to look embarrassed. "Once, twice a year."

"And never to see us? Dad, Evan, me?"

"No. I felt, shall we say, guilty, each time. So this is why I came now."

"Do you have any idea why someone is targeting you, your family?" Malcolm wanted to keep Aksel on track, and he was here now. He and Jade could reminisce when this was all over.

And Malcolm didn't have to witness it.

Aksel shrugged as only the French can do. "No, Gerard and my father were painters, actually living where I now live. They taught at the École des Beaux-Arts, and that's where Evan met them."

"Where are you staying now?"

"With an old friend. It's a safe place."

"Does this friend have any kind of security?" Malcolm rapid-fired his questions.

"Yes."

"And?" Jade motioned with her hands for him to clarify.

Aksel turned from Malcolm to give Jade a small smile at her interruption. "I promise to be as safe as possible until this person is caught. No more sitting on porches or hanging around the Pearl Street Mall. I have a lot of reading to catch up on." He turned back to face Malcolm. "Will that do, Talbot?"

"Just remember, Jade needs her family."

Malcolm intercepted her grateful look over his gentle warning. It should have warmed him except for the guilt he harbored over the indisputable fact that somehow the killer was one step ahead of him and his team. He turned to Aksel. "You should take every precaution. The security here is tight, but someone still managed to get inside."

The message on Jade's mirror had shaken him. *How did that bastard get in? No evidence of a break in, so the only way was through his security. How? Jade's phone?*

"I can't stay here, Malcolm. I can't." Jade wrapped her arms around her midriff as if holding herself together.

Her beseeching gaze painted his mood blacker. Then she grasped his arm as if to reinforce her request, expressing her need to be gone from the one place she'd felt was a safe harbor. His intent to make her secure here hadn't worked. In fact, it was a spectacular failure.

Tamping down both frustration and anger, he composed his face into what he hoped was a steady and confident look. "I've already made new plans—"

The detectives returned from outside and approached Malcolm. "We're done here. There were three sets of fingerprints on the security panel." Tomba interrupted in his tough cop voice.

Someone very knowledgeable had done this. The system his crew had installed was quite sophisticated. Malcolm ground his teeth. "A couple will be my techs'. I'll send you their prints. And mine."

"Then we'll just need yours, Mr. Basarias, and yours, Ms. Laurent."

Aksel inclined his head.

"I'll send in Jade's with ours."

Tomba gave him a long stare. Malcolm matched it. He wasn't going to subject Jade to fingerprinting or dealing with these men. They were good at their jobs, played good cop–bad cop well, but he knew Jade had nothing to do with this. Evan Fischer's leaving everything to Jade made sense. The detectives knew they were reaching and were simply following their protocol. Well, so was he.

Malcolm had just secured a new safehouse for him and Jade, and he wasn't planning on leaving it except to go to Evan's house and quickly retrieve that envelope Jade mentioned. He was now both bodyguard and PI. Something he'd tried to avoid.

Furthermore, after this latest breach and threat and how shaken it left her, he was sure he'd not have any further arguments from Jade about going with him to Evan's. The new safehouse was just that, safe.

"Ms. Laurent, please don't leave town," Moore cautioned in a much calmer voice than Tomba was using with Jade.

"No problem, she'll be with me."

Brows raised, Aksel looked from him to her and back to Malcolm as the detectives left the house. Then with his elegant shrug, which Malcolm was coming to hate, he smiled at Jade and followed the detectives out.

8

WHILE IT HADN'T TAKEN JADE LONG TO THROW CLOTHES AND toiletries into a satchel to take to the new location, Malcolm told her they needed to wait an hour before they headed out.

With only the two of them left in her house, and Malcolm working his phone, not talking, the minutes passed in agonizing slowness. And as much as Jade usually loved the mantel clock, its ticking annoyed her to the point of putting it inside a kitchen cupboard.

Her skin crawled at the slightest of noises. She felt hyper aware and couldn't seem to control her breathing. Fast to normal to fast again.

And when Malcolm did look up from his phone, he watched her like an eagle, unnerving her more. What did he think she was going to do, run away?

Silly girl, maybe he's just concerned about you.

Finally he got whatever message he'd been waiting for, and they were on their way to new, thoroughly vetted digs. Something she'd refused to do only three days ago. But now Mike had a nephew at risk, Aksel was a target, and somebody had been able to breach the vaunted security rigged at her home.

"Ready?"

"Yes."

"Would you please carry the satchel, so I can be hands-free to ..."

She hoisted the bag over her shoulder and nodded, not needing him to finish his sentence. She knew he meant so he could grab his weapon if needed.

They hustled out to his Range Rover and Malcolm backed out of her driveway quickly.

She looked back to see her home disappear in the distance.

Home. Would she ever feel safe there again? So much of her life was irrevocably changed that the deep sadness which had damaged her core felt permanent.

She finally summoned the energy to turn her head and focus on him. His jaw was clenched and his hands held the steering wheel so tightly his knuckles almost protruded through his skin. And worse, he seemed more distant than he had before this whole freaking nightmare started. It wasn't his fault. Nobody was invincible.

Not knowing what to say to ease his strain, she said nothing and instead tried to banish her own fog of misery, hoping that would help.

Paying attention to where they were driving, she was surprised when Malcolm turned off Baseline Road onto 15th Street. She was sure they were headed out of Boulder. They wound through the streets of the neighborhood directly east of Chautauqua Park, then started climbing a small narrow road up the back side of Enchanted Mesa.

Malcolm drove slowly, scanning the roads below, looking for, she assumed, a tail of some sort. He finally pulled into the long, curving driveway of a magnificent house Jade had admired for years when she'd hiked on some of Chautauqua's many trails.

The driveway held a Tesla SUV. One man stood at the garage and waved. She craned her neck to see another man on the pool deck built into the side of the mesa. She realized immediately he had a good vantage point and was watching the road as Malcolm had done. As they approached the garage, the man by the pool glanced back at them, gave a thumbs up, and flashed her a brief smile.

She couldn't help but return it.

The tall man at the garage pushed something, and the garage door opened. It housed a powerful-looking black BMW SUV. Malcolm pulled in next to it, and the man slipped inside as the garage door closed immediately.

She felt like she was in a James Bond movie. Stealth and mum's the word.

That made her think British, and immediately Mrs. Cole came to mind. She needed to know how the older woman was faring and made a mental note in her swiss cheese brain to ask Malcolm if she could call the hospital. Then she realized they wouldn't tell her anything. But David might.

The man helped Jade out of the Range Rover, clasped Malcolm's hand in greeting, and shepherded them into the house.

They entered right into the main room of the house. A woman stood at the north-facing wall of windows. She didn't turn to greet them, just steadily kept watch.

How many employees did Malcolm have? And did they all work using telepathy or secret hand signals? Not a word had been uttered.

The man who had met them at the entrance checked his phone. "So far so good."

As Jade watched, Malcolm's ramrod, stress-induced posture relaxed.

She felt his hand on her back, gently pushing her further into the room.

"Jade, this is Jason St. Pierre. His wife, Catherine Hemstead St. Pierre, is the lookout at the window. I'm guessing Haley, their daughter, will make an appearance soon."

Jason nodded and smiled.

It was as if a ray of sunshine flooded the room. He radiated friendliness and oddly she felt as if she'd known him forever.

"The man on the pool deck is Gus Tanaka. All of us are friends who offered help," Jason said with a gentle tone.

Sudden tears flooded her eyes and she dashed them away. "Thank you so much for all this. It's unbelievably generous of you. But are you putting yourselves at risk?" She looked at Malcolm, then Jason. "Mrs. St. Pierre?"

"No, we're not." Catherine St. Pierre turned from her spot at the window and held out her hand. "Call me Cate, please. We'll be fine," she stated, voice firm with confidence.

A bit of which seeped into Jade.

"The pantry is stocked. We're meeting the delivery guy in a bit and will bring back the perishables. Then the house is yours and Malcolm's. Let me show you your bedroom."

Totally inappropriate images flitted through her mind at Cate's inadvertent sandwiching of words, *house, yours and Malcolm's, your bedroom.* Jade blinked, hoping that would clear her mind. What the heck was wrong with her? This was a life and death struggle right now, and she was having fantasy thoughts?

Give yourself a break, girl. That is exactly why—it's a release. You're not going to be lovers, ever. Simple. It was just a release.

Jade followed Cate past a long but low stone wall built in the house, acting like a corridor to what Jade could only imagine was the master bedroom. "Shower, change, and take a nap if you want. We're not leaving for a bit. Our house is your house. Malcolm is ohana to us and so are you."

"Ohana?"

"Family."

Tears flooded Jade's eyes and blurred her vision. A tinier version of Cate stood in the doorway. This must be Haley. She plucked something off the bureau and handed it to Jade. A tissue.

"This is our daughter, Haley."

"Thank you, Haley." Jade's eyes filled again at the sweet gesture from the child.

"If Mommy and Daddy say you're ohana, then you are. I'm happy to have another aunty."

"Aunty?"

"What kids in Hawaii call their friends' parents or close elders," Cate explained.

"Can I hug her, Mommy?"

"It's up to Jade."

She nodded. Haley gently wrapped her arms around her waist and squeezed oh-so-carefully. Jade did the same, and they stood that way for only a few seconds, but Jade felt the connection as if this group of people had been in her life forever. "Ohana."

Haley backed away to stand by her mother, who smiled, and they left the room to Jade.

How had Malcolm known that these people, this place, were exactly what she needed?

Putting her bag on the bed's silky, celery-green duvet, she sat next to it and let the room's soft greens, peaches, and hint of old-Hawaii-inspired décor sink into her soul. Windows faced east, and the sun warmed the room. Too emotionally drained to move more than her head, she turned to look behind her, seeing an old Hawaiian quilt gracing the wall over the bed. The minimal furniture in the room was crafted from dark-hued koa wood.

Unpacking her satchel, Jade placed her simple clothing in one of the low wooden dressers. In this nurturing environment, the tension of the last few days slowly drained from her, leaving her exhausted. Then, summoning the last bit of energy she possessed, knowing a shower would help ease her anxiety, she headed into the bathroom.

Designed with black, beiges, and splashes of a persimmon color, the bathroom had the Zen feeling of a spa. Stripping, she entered the massive glass-enclosed shower. Playing with the dials, she let the warm water from the rain shower head pour slowly over her. Finally feeling energetic enough to scrub her hair and body, she turned on another set of jets and went to it. It was cathartic to wash away the last hours of pure madness. From Mrs. Cole's collapse and her odd mention of her son David, almost implicating him somehow, to the breach of her house, and then the deadly message scrawled across her mirror.

Not knowing how long she'd been in this little slice of heaven, sure it had been a good while though, and unbelievably the hot water kept on coming, she decided she was ready to face whatever Malcolm thought should happen next.

Knowing him, it would mean nothing she could participate in.

Right this second, that was okay. Too many crises in three days. Tomorrow she'd figure out a way to convince him that being a part of this was still vital to her.

Wrapping a fluffy bath sheet around her released a scent of something lightly floral that only enhanced her feeling of security. She entered the bedroom to find a tray with a carafe of coffee, a bowl of sliced kiwi, orange, and pear, and beside it, a small bowl of assorted nuts. Heaven.

Sitting cross-legged on the bed, she wolfed down the fruit, then nibbled on the nuts between leisurely sips of the coffee. The vast king bed invited taking a nap, and she almost gave in to the urge. Instead, she poured more caffeine.

Finishing her second cup and feeling caffeinated enough to face her hosts and Malcolm, she looked at her meager selection of clothes and decided on jeans, a navy fleece top, then threw on her laceless canvas tennies. A quick swipe of mascara and a finger brush of her hair and she was ready. Gathering up the tray, she retraced her steps and found Haley in one corner of the living room. The little girl sat in a bean bag chair, reading a book, wearing headphones with a scruffy pink bunny propped up next to her. Malcolm, Jason, Cate, and the slim Asian man by the pool Malcolm had called Gus Tanaka were seated around the kitchen counter.

Gus rose from his seat and enveloped her in a gentle hug.

"Jade, Gus is the brains behind our new group of confederates," Jason said.

"Right behind you, bro." Gus winked.

"He was key in getting Haley back to us last year," Cate added.

Jade swiveled between all of them as they raved about Gus.

And what was this story about getting Haley back?

"He actually came to the mainland for a bit of vacation and to work on recruiting me to be part of his new idea," Jason clarified. "Now I think he's going to try and recruit Harrison and Talbot as well."

Jade looked at Gus. "For what?"

"I want to build a network of private investigators and experts in their field. Specialized work. I'm calling it The Kahuna Group."

Jade felt a glimmer of an idea flash. Her pulse quickened and the shroud of darkness lifted a bit. This wasn't the time, but she was sure Malcolm could help her with this nugget of an idea. "Jason, are you a PI as well?"

He laughed gently. "No way. I don't have that kind of skill set. But computers, finance, and media I can help with."

"In other words, my brother from a different mother has the brains, money, and connections to make this all work," Gus said, then smiled broadly.

"Ohana," Jade said softly.

Gus nodded. Then Cate, Jason, and Malcolm did the same. "You're never without family, Jade," Gus said.

Her shroud lifted more.

Gus got off the stool, followed by Cate and Jason. "We're heading out. Malcolm will go over all the codes with you, and we'll meet again, soon, eh?"

Cate went over to Haley, who, without a fuss, put her book and earphones in her backpack, tucked her bunny under her arm and joined the group waiting at the door. Each one gave Jade a soft hug. "Aloha, Jade," Gus said as he closed the door behind him.

And she was left with Malcolm. In a new safehouse. Alone.

This felt much different from when she stayed at his condo, which had also only been the two of them, but that time, shock had reigned supreme. She was still afraid, but other emotions were beginning to surface. Even a sense of looking forward to the future.

A huge yawn escaped before she could hold it in.

"Food or nap? Cate ordered enough food for a small army. I was going to make some soup and a sandwich to split. And I want to give you the alarm codes to the house."

Jade searched Malcolm's face for some hint of how he felt.

She'd put him through so much more than he could have bargained for.

"I had the fruit Cate brought in, and even several cups of coffee aren't keeping me awake. So it's a nap for me, but go ahead and eat. I'll see you in an hour or so, and I'm sure then I'll eat Cate out of house and home. I feel even more guilty they're having to leave."

"Jade, this isn't where they live. They have a house in Morrison and a condo on Oahu. And this. Marta lives here when she's not traveling solo or with Cate, Jason, and Haley. Right now, she happens to be at their condo in Hawaii."

"Wow. And who is this Marta?"

"Jason's right-hand woman. She keeps everything in his life on track. Now that Cate and Jason are married ..."

"Wait—"

"I'll explain it all later. They had a complicated route to finally end up where they are."

Jade was going to say more, but another yawn took the words from her. "Can I wait to learn the codes for the alarm?" She bit off the "please" at the end, knowing it would have sounded whiney.

Malcolm nodded. "Have a good nap."

She stood and for a millisecond she wanted to give him the same gentle hug she'd received from the ohana moments ago. Instead, uncertain how Malcolm would react, she turned away, only to be stopped by his hand on her arm.

Turning back, he was so close, nearly touching her. Giving in to the need to be connected, if only for a brief moment, she put her arms around him. Instantly he drew her closer so that her cheek rested on his chest. She heard his heartbeat, felt his warmth, and cherished the fact that he was willing to give comfort. And realized that he had offered just that, practically from the moment he'd been involved in this whole insane mess.

Remaining in his arms was impossible. Jade pulled away from the safety of his embrace and back to reality.

"Thank you," she said softly, then headed to her bedroom for the nap she so desperately needed, wondering if it would be just sleep or dreams of the man who was protecting her.

9

A KEENING WAIL RIPPED THROUGH THE HOUSE. MALCOLM launched himself off the kitchen stool and was in Jade's bedroom in seconds.

She scrabbled at the sheets as she twisted, apparently trying to get away from whoever was chasing her in her dreams.

Malcolm gathered her against him, realizing as he held her that she'd stripped to a T-shirt with nothing on beneath except scraps of lace that passed for panties. He ignored her state of undress, wanting only to comfort her. "Shush, it's just a dream. I've got you, you're safe," he crooned over and over as he stroked her hair, her cheeks, until her trembling slowed.

"He had Haley and Cate and then you and he told me ... I had the choice. Me or them. Then he laughed, saying all would die anyway no matter ... what I chose. Malcolm, everyone would d-die."

She breathed rapidly between each word and tears streaked her cheeks, bruising his own heart. "Honey, it's just a bad dream. You found a new family and you were projecting. Relax, I've got you," he said as he cradled her, gently rubbing her back, aware that he was in way over his rigid "no emotional involvement" with clients policy.

Oddly, he didn't want to go back to being strictly client/PI. What was it about this petite woman that made him want more?

Jade was fierce, loyal, a warrior. Yet he sensed a yearning under her veneer of being an astute businesswoman. Her dream almost indicated that she wanted the comfort of family, yet something held her back. She dated, but it didn't sound serious with David Cole. She had made it sound like her dates were a marker in time. Something to do until she ... what? That was the million-dollar question, and Malcolm wanted to find the answer.

She sniffled and let loose a deep, heavy sigh. "You're good at this comforting job."

"I had a lot of practice."

"How?"

"Brothers." Malcolm didn't even deliberate the pros and cons of confiding a bit of his life. He did have a life outside of Harrison & Talbot, just a very limited one. Dates with women who were no more interested in a long relationship than he was. Megan and Greg. Jason, Cate, Haley, and Gus. That was the extent of his friends.

He wanted Jade to know more about him to see if they could ... what? Be friends? That was another million-dollar question. Pushing aside that line of thought, he continued his answer. "Yep, three brothers who think I'm overprotective."

"Imagine that. So you're the oldest. What are their names?"

"Samuel, William, and John—or various nicknames, depending on the circumstances."

"Do they look like you?"

"Nah, not as handsome by far." He felt her punch his arm. "Seriously, John has a slightly crooked nose from a break when he was a sophomore in high school."

"How?" Jade snuggled deeper against him, so she was half sitting on his lap. He didn't have the heart or the desire to move her away, instead he shifted a bit so they were comfortable. He wrapped his arm around her to hold her close.

He rested his chin on the top of her head and stared at the far wall in front of the bed, letting its blankness be a screen for the memory. "I was eighteen. My brother, who was on the JV squad baseball team, had been hit in the face with a wild pitch. He was on the way to the ER.

"They tried calling home, but no one answered. The principal remembered my name, found my class, and told me. He offered me his car as I didn't have one, but I was too worried, not in control, so I asked him to drive me to the hospital.

"I waited long hours as families came and went, mothers and fathers taking care of their children, until the surgeon came out to tell me that my brother had been lucky. He didn't have any brain damage from his crushed septum. The bone fragments hadn't penetrated the blood veil, but he would need some reconstructive surgery. It could be done right away if I could get a parental signature."

Malcolm glanced down at Jade. Her face was upturned, watching him, her brow furrowed with concentration even as her eyes softened with compassion.

"I explained there wasn't a parent who was coherent enough to sign anything. No matter how much I argued with the doctor, I couldn't get past the system. I hadn't even wanted my brother to try out for baseball because of this very reason. It can be a dangerous sport."

"You were being overprotective," Jade said, her voice soft.

"My brothers will tell you I still am."

"So why wasn't your mom or dad at the hospital?"

Malcolm thought he'd be vague with his reply, yet the true

answer begged for release. "Remember I said there wasn't a parent coherent enough at that time?"

Malcolm didn't wait for her nod. The words burst from him. "Mom died in childbirth years before, and Dad, well ..." Malcolm shrugged. "He never forgave himself. Of course, it wasn't his fault, but he loved her with such desperation, such devotion, that he lost all reason to function. He tried to bury his pain in alcohol and other women. He worked when he was able.

"He left me and my brothers pretty much alone. As eldest, I became both father and mother, both disciplinarian and holder of dreams. I wanted to be a lawyer, to hold all that was just up to the righteousness of the law. Well, the law isn't just, or I should say, the law as interpreted often isn't just.

"About the time I discovered that I needed to be on a different team, my bros were entering college. Nevertheless, I left law and started the agency with Greg, giving as much as I could spare financially to the masses, as my siblings call themselves."

His brothers often accused him of smothering them when he'd only wanted to keep them from the pain he'd experienced. It hadn't worked. Nevertheless, in spite of their differences, they'd all gone on to build successful careers, found women of their own, and started families.

They nurtured healthy love.

Only Malcolm had remained the lone holdout against love and commitment. Despite the need buried deep in his heart to have what his brothers had, he wasn't going to risk the horrible pain that love lost could bring.

Yet holding this woman who had been fiercely strong and who he knew was loyal to a fault, feeling her understanding and her strength, he knew if circumstances were different, he'd have the answer to what he wanted. His petite warrior by his side.

"I'd love to meet your family someday," Jade said.

There was no mistaking the wistfulness in her voice, revealing a part of her heart. They both wanted someone close, someone to be a partner with.

Someone to love.

But circumstances *weren't* different and the timing wrong.

It was time to finish the story, and he still didn't regret revealing a part of himself. "Meeting the masses, yes—Dad, no. He went for a drive one day and didn't come home. I think he planned it that way. He was done living."

Jade's sniffle caught him by surprise, as did the tears sliding down her cheeks. "Ah, honey, I didn't mean for you to cry more. I should have thought before I spoke." He thumbed the wetness away.

"These are tears for you, not for me," she said softly.

He bent, kissing her the top of her head, his lips on silky hair.

They could have spent all afternoon wrapped in the still harmony of the moment.

Until Jade's stomach rumbled.

JADE SAT AT THE KITCHEN ISLAND, RUNNING HER HAND OVER THE cool, highly polished cement surface. As she watched Malcolm reheat soup and build a sandwich for the two of them to share, she imagined the whole Kahuna Group gathered around the counter, laughing, sharing stories ... being ohana.

She felt different. About so many things.

Malcolm. She could never go back to thinking he was solely a pain in the tuchus, bossing her around, even though it was for her own good.

He'd called her "honey," and something between them had shifted.

Yet, from the story and the revelations he'd made, she knew he was going to keep her as safe as possible *in* this house. And a tiny part of her wanted to be tucked away and safe. But the key to the horror of what was happening could be found outside these walls at Evan's. She needed to find the envelope that he'd made such a priority in case something did happen to him.

So being stuck here wasn't acceptable. There had to be a way to convince Malcolm.

And while in his arms, listening to his story about his starting in one career and realizing something other than that called to him gave a name to why she'd been so antsy in her skin for the last year since her father's death. She was inhabiting a persona that was no longer hers.

She'd been swaddled by both Evan and her father. Always told just enough to make their point, and frankly it was partially her fault as well. She hadn't asked deeper questions, content with the status quo. Not knowing what else she wanted. Not taking the time to question herself deeply.

Evan hadn't told her why couriering the Khan could be dangerous. He just took over. Just as her father refused to tell her about her mother and what happened to their relationship. Keeping her in the dark, protecting her, had been a pattern. And now the three men who were friends were dead, and she had no idea why. She should have asked more questions.

A mistake she wouldn't repeat.

Nor would she allow anyone to shatter her new idea. When Gus had chatted about his idea of building a network of private investigators that were experts in their field, he'd planted the seeds for a new direction her life could take.

She was an art expert and there was a lot of fraud in the art world. Always had been. However, the values for original works were now astronomical, and buyers needed proof of authenticity. If a painting wasn't genuine, then tracking down the source of the forgery sounded like a job right up her alley.

When the moment was right, she'd talk to Malcolm about her idea. After all, Gus wanted him in the Kahuna Group. But right now, the sense of excitement coursing through her was liberating and energizing enough.

And if Malcolm wouldn't help her, maybe Gus would.

But you want Malcolm on your side, by your side.

Yes, but you know that love controls. It doesn't free a person.

Her swaddling clothes had been ripped off these last four days, and she was now raw and tender.

And free.

She wasn't going to allow Malcolm to wrap her back up in cotton wool. And she knew he'd want to.

Just then the man who dominated her thoughts turned from the stove and centered a grilled ham and cheese half sandwich on a plate beside a mug of steaming soup in front of her.

"I didn't realize how hungry I am. This smells gourmet." She could barely wait to dig in as the tangy scent of tomato basil soup mingled with hot ham, rich browned swiss cheese on sourdough toast grilled in butter fired up her taste buds.

He put a mug of soup and another plate with his half of the sandwich on the counter, then came around and sat on the stool beside her.

For minutes, the only sound in the big room was the meal being savored.

Finally Jade slowed down and actually chewed before she swallowed. "Did you bribe your brothers with food to make them behave?"

"Nope, I threatened them with KP duty. It worked every time."

"You didn't do all the chores around the house, did you?"

"We had a rotating duty list. And actually, the guys became

pretty proficient cooks. For which their wives are eternally grateful to me."

"Lean forward."

He did, and she dabbed at a bit of cheese clinging to his lips, then wondered what made her make such an intimate gesture.

Time to get back to neutral ground, girl.

"Do they live in Colorado?" Jade asked, as she thought back and couldn't recall Megan ever mentioning Malcolm's family to her.

"No, and I don't see them enough. Partially—no, wholly—my fault."

Jade sipped the soup again, watching him over the rim of her mug. Their gazes caught and held. She saw a flicker of tenderness that echoed her gesture of moments ago.

Which made her next request all the more difficult, as the harmony between them was a balm to her raw and newly born state of independence.

She waited until he took his last bite of sandwich and swallowed.

"Malcolm—"

"You want to go to Evan's with me?"

She nodded.

"You know, if I could, I'd leave you here, locked inside."

Jade searched his face for his old, shuttered look, relieved it wasn't there. "But you won't."

"No. Though it's against my better judgement."

"You'll be right beside me."

For a second uncertainty flickered in his gaze before he looked down at his plate.

Jade wasn't sure she hadn't imagined it. "I also need to go to the office."

That brought his head back up and their gazes locked.

"With Megan," she added.

"Because?"

She couldn't stop her deep sigh, but he needed to know exactly why. "News will come out about the Khan, and clients will be worried. Besides, we've never closed the business without notice. We've been unavailable for four days now, including today, a Saturday. I don't know how to work the computer system to look at the upcoming contracts, and we need to be in touch with those customers. The phone message indicated we'd be closed through the weekend, but if clients try and get in touch and can't on Monday, it could worry them to the point of breaking their contract. After all, we're talking large amounts of money. I won't give up Laurent's stellar reputation without a fight."

"Let's tackle one job at a time and see how it plays out, okay? Right now, let's head to Evan's before the daylight fades."

Lifting her chin, pulling up the Laurent pride, she inclined her head once, almost regally.

And got a chuckle.

10

JADE'S NEWFOUND STRENGTH EBBED AS THEY GOT CLOSER TO Evan's house. "The next one on the right," she directed Malcolm.

He pulled the decoy vehicle, Marta's black BMW, to a stop at the curb. For a long moment Jade stared at the small, pale-yellow bungalow that had always brought a smile to her face, especially the front door and shutters. Painted not just blue, but a phthalo blue. An artist's color.

Nothing looked different from the last time she'd been there, but she felt the home that had been Evan's for multiple decades knew its owner wasn't coming back.

Pushing the fanciful notion aside, she saw some of his meticulous landscaping was beginning to emerge. Soon the yellows of forsythia, multicolored crocus planted in large swathes, and the small Japanese maple would be a riot of an almost modernistic palette as the front yard plants moved through the seasons.

His backyard was planted to bring all the colors of a Monet watercolor to life. He even had a small lily pond, though no bridge. And a large weeping willow tree that he had meticulously trimmed every year.

Abruptly she turned away from the falsely idyllic scene. Evan wasn't going to open the door and beckon her inside. "Nothing is going to be the same without him."

Sorrow thickened her voice and she clasped her hands tightly, fighting for control. Jade didn't think she had another tear to shed, and more than being dry eyed, she needed to be stronger than her grief and help find the madman who wanted to snuff out her life as well. She took a deep, jagged breath.

"You're sure you want to do this?" Malcolm asked, using a gentle tone.

"Yes. We need that letter Evan told me to retrieve. It's got to hold a key to some of this madness."

Braving his searching gaze, she pulled up that tenuous thread of strength, knowing he could see right through her bravado. "Malcolm, let me edit that last statement. I couldn't do this if you weren't here, beside me."

He reached across the center console and, with the back of his fingers, lightly stroked her cheek. "You're brave, Jade Laurent. We'll get through this and then the next step until we solve this."

He turned off the engine and started to open the BMW's door.

Jade touched his arm, stopping him. "Thank you for saying 'we.'"

He grinned. "Not much choice given me, right?"

"Right."

"Okay, got the key out?"

"Yes. Got the gun?"

His gaze sharpened. "Yep. Walk quickly, get inside, then no matter what, lock the door behind you."

MALCOLM STOOD IN THE MIDDLE OF EVAN'S SMALL FOYER, holding Jade's arm and looking at the completely trashed living room. She leaned heavily against him, fist to her mouth. Trembling, not in fear but in rage.

Oriental carpets heaped in piles, their tumbled, vibrant colors reminding him of a giant finger painting all over the floor. Sofa cushions had been shredded, their foam stuffing spilling from the gashes. The expensive-looking prints that once graced the walls were now ripped apart and scattered on the floor.

This felt like an act of revenge, not a simple break-in. He sniffed the air. "Did Evan smoke?"

"No, but I smell it too. Did the idiot smoke while he trashed Evan's house?"

"I'm guessing this was his or her first mistake. Who do you know that smokes?"

Jade turned toward him slowly. Malcolm waited. She knew someone, he could tell by the uncomfortable look on her face. "David Cole. He vapes. He's been trying to quit."

"I don't know if vaping would put out this kind of pungent tobacco smell. But I'll look into it." He looked down at her. "We're going to check out the rooms. I want you to follow me, move when I do until I know for sure it's clear. Not hearing anything is a good sign, but we're here now, and whoever broke in could be hiding."

Pulling his gun, he held it downward, at ready, in a two-fisted grip, finger off the trigger. Thankfully Jade didn't offer any argument over his orders.

Malcolm led the way as they moved through the living room into a hallway.

"Bedrooms are on that side, facing the garden," she said from behind him. "Studio office on this side, and the kitchen along the back, facing the driveway. Odd arrangement, but Evan never wanted to make those huge structural changes."

She pointed toward a door. "First one is a bathroom. Second one is his bedroom."

Malcolm signaled for Jade to stand to one side as he opened each door. The bath and bedroom were as neat as a pin. Swiftly he checked Evan's closet, and it was as ordered as his own.

As they were about to enter the den-slash-office, a loud rapping on the front door caught Malcolm completely by surprise. Pivoting on a dime, together they fast-walked to the front door.

Using an abundance of caution, he moved to the side of the door, aware that more people got shot standing directly behind the door. And with Jade still right behind him, he stretched and looked out the peep hole. A woman wearing a turquoise-colored jogging suit stood there, hands on her hips.

"Do you know a tall woman with curly, shoulder-length gray hair?" Malcolm whispered.

"Yes, Evan's next-door neighbor."

"Evan, you're not answering your phone and the first batch is done. You promised to come over at four," the woman said loudly.

"Oh, yes, that is certainly Mrs. Smith. We've had coffee over there several times. She's a gossip, but a great baker."

"Good, then she knows you. Put on your acting shoes. Tell her Evan is sick, and you'll get together later."

The rapping started again.

Jade opened the door as Malcolm stood behind her, blocking any view into the trashed living room, his gun still held downward. Just in case the woman was a hostage.

"Jade, hello. I saw you both come over."

"Mrs. Smith, how nice to see you. Evan caught something and he's not well at all. I–we were just checking on him. Can we get together next week?"

"Of course, but why don't I run over and get a batch of my bars for him and you and your, uh, friend as well."

Malcolm caught her eying him over Jade's head and offered an easy smile.

"How about tomorrow. I hear him ... calling. Later then. I'll tell him you stopped by."

"Okay." Mrs. Smith turned away, then turned back. "Then I'm guessing that wasn't his motorcycle I saw earlier. I was beginning to think he'd lost his mind. Tell him—"

"What motorcycle?" Malcolm moved forward enough so she could see him clearly, his weapon still hidden.

She frowned at his interruption and he shrugged an apology. "Just curious. A bike cut us off at the intersection, and I thought it could be the same one."

"Oh yes, I hate it when they do that. It was big. It pulled out of Evan's driveway as I was standing at my kitchen window making another cup of coffee."

"When was this?"

"Maybe three hours, ago. I have to think back, it was my third batch—"

"Can you describe the bike?"

"Sure. I'm known for my eagle eyes. Red Ducati, no license plate though. The rider had a helmet on. Basic black biker gear. Oh, and there was a logo on the gas tank."

"What did it look like?" Jade asked.

"Half of a globe made up of varying shades of blue dots with initials in the other half."

"Eagle eyes, indeed, Mrs. Smith." Damn, the same bike that cut them off two days ago in Denver. "Yup, that was the one we saw," Malcolm said. He touched Jade's back, hoping she got his message about wrapping this up.

"I gotta go check on Evan. We'll take a raincheck on the

granola bars, 'K?" Jade waved as she closed the door and slumped against it.

"You want another career? Try acting. You were great."

"You mean you couldn't see my hands trembling and hear my knees knocking?"

"Nope." Malcolm winked at her. "Oscar-worthy performance." The wink earned him a quick grin.

"It was the same bike," she said in measured tones.

Malcolm nodded as he holstered his weapon for the time being. He got the sense that no one else was in house. Whoever trashed the place left on that bike.

"And we're only about three hours late."

"I'm surprised he wasn't here right after Evan's ... death. But being here just hours before us is more his MO. Somehow he knows what you're doing. And he's taunting you."

"The only thing I've had the entire time is my cell phone and my purse."

Malcolm scanned the tossed room, seeing no surface that was flat or clear enough for them to sit. The only option was the foyer floor. He sat, patting the space next to him. "Would you empty your purse of absolutely everything? Even the lipstick tubes," he added with a light tone. For both their sakes he hoped to God he'd find something, and if he did, he'd be incredibly furious with himself.

He went through everything, all the pockets outside and in. Nothing that resembled a tracker or a bug was in there. "Okay, now your phone."

She unlocked it and handed it over. Malcolm scanned all her apps, not many actually, and punched in a few codes to check for hidden apps. Nothing. "It looks clean to me. Ready to investigate the rest of the house?" The relief he felt at not finding anything was instantly tempered by the fact that he still didn't know how this idiot was one step ahead of them. He'd watched for tails since the morgue, and other than the obvious moves by the motorcycle rider in Denver letting him know he was onto them, he'd seen nothing.

"Yes. I'm ready for anything that will bring this nightmare to a close," she said, voice strong.

Jade was again in her petite warrior mode. He wondered if he'd ever get the chance to tell her his nickname for her. And realized he hoped the answer was affirmative. But now was the time to find the folder with the letter Evan had told Jade was so important.

He stood and held out a hand to Jade, hauling her to her feet. "Kitchen next and then Evan's office."

He reached the kitchen door and looked in. The bright room was surprisingly neat, almost perfect. Too perfect. It didn't fit with the rest of the destruction. He even detected the faint odor of cleaning chemicals. His hair stood up, and he held his finger to his lips, signaling the need for silence.

He pulled out his gun, and they moved into the kitchen. Jade stopped just inside the door so she couldn't be grabbed from behind.

Malcolm quickly inspected the door lock, and it didn't look jimmied either. Nor was the glass broken in the top half of the door. Nevertheless, the kitchen felt disturbed. From what he'd seen of the mess in the rest of the house, this tidiness was odd. "This is the only other way into the house, right?"

She nodded.

"Then whomever did the mess in the living room had a key. This wasn't a random break-in."

He made sure she was behind him as he opened to door to the last room. Evan's study.

~

MALCOLM WASN'T MOVING, HADN'T SAID A WORD SINCE OPENING the door. Jade shifted just enough to give her a view of what turned him to stone.

"The bastard," she growled. Bile rose in her throat, scorching it with acid over the complete upheaval and destruction in Evan's office.

One uncompleted painting standing on an easel had been slashed viciously, and tubes of paint from the taboret nearby had been squeezed over the canvas and squirted on the white walls.

Evan's cherry desk was overturned, its drawers haphazardly thrown about. The drawers from the small filing cabinet suffered the same fate. Papers littered the floor as if someone threw them in the air and they landed wherever.

"This had to have taken more than a few hours." Her voice shook with rage.

"Not if the person knew they were looking for a specific file. The rest could just be fury-driven destruction. There is no place for a person to hide here. I'm getting the sense he wanted you to see this. He's toying with you."

She saw Malcolm pull two pairs of nitrile gloves from a pocket inside his jacket. "You come prepared."

"I've got more stuff in these pockets than you can imagine."

She slowly scanned him, not seeing any kind of bulges that would indicate anything other than the gun in its belt holster, and that was because she knew it was there.

"It's the art of packing," he said. "Gloves, plastic ties—"

"Why the gloves?"

"Because you may want to call this is in as a B&E when we're done. Your fingerprints will be expected, mine are on a few knobs, and I can explain that away. But we don't want them on any of this paperwork."

She surveyed the room, her heart breaking into more pieces. The paint on the walls was beginning to dry. "I didn't realize he'd started to paint again. That was his primary reason for moving to Tuscany. He said the light was nearly always perfect. He wasn't going total ex-pat. He thought he'd find renters for this house, and then in a couple of years he'd decide where he'd spend the rest of his days."

The deep sigh came straight from her core. "I don't even know where to start with this mess."

"You take the area around the desk, and I'll start here at the doorway and we'll work toward the middle. But first, let's right this desk—do you think you can lift one side?"

"I may be height-challenged, but I've got muscles."

After setting the desk upright and trying to think like Evan, she methodically turned over each desk drawer and looked at the bottom, just to see if anything was taped there. Nothing, not even any residue. Replacing each drawer after checking its cubby made the task seem a tiny bit less daunting, though it did nothing to lessen her fury.

She held on to the black emotion as it was better than the deep sadness and fear that had filled her the past four days.

Sitting on the floor, her back against the desk, she scooped up a pile of papers and file folders. Their labels would help with sorting.

Topping the pile was a folder labeled Basarias. For a moment she was puzzled by it. Why would Evan have a folder for his friend? But she quickly realized it made sense. After all, Omarr, Evan, and her father Gerard had been a trio long before she and Aksel had come along. Before Mère—the name her mother demanded she use—left and Omarr's beloved wife, Heloise, died.

Not immediately finding anything more than would appear

to be in that file, she felt keen disappointment slice into her fury-driven adrenaline.

Then, as if Evan were standing beside her, she heard his voice.

"You are strong, Jade Laurent. You can move to the top of the pack if that's what you want. You simply have to be smarter than the next guy and watch your back."

He'd told her this about a month after her father was struck and killed. She was sitting in the firm's inner office on her side of the desk facing the empty chair when Evan walked in, closed the door, and sat in her father's place. *"Most importantly, believe in your inner guide. That's never led you astray."*

She thought of her burgeoning idea and wondered what Evan would have thought.

"Most importantly, believe in your inner guide. That's never led you astray" played again in her mind. And gave her confidence ... until her practical voice added the word "yet" to Evan's pep talk.

Right now, everything seemed impossible, including this monumental task in front of her. Glancing up, she realized Malcolm had gone through more of his pile than she had of hers. He was moving closer to the center of the room, and yet his piles were methodical and precise.

She quickly picked up her pace, skimmed each page, and piled them up the way he did—after all, he was the PI. And reading each page thoroughly, going through the hard copy of Evan's life was too emotional. She needed to be clear-eyed about this. Detailed reading could come later. Much later.

"Jade, what is nephrite?" Malcolm asked.

"Jade," she said, not looking up from her new pile.

"Yup, that's your name."

"What are you talking about?"

"This."

She looked up to see Malcolm in front of her, waving a

manila folder. "It's labeled Nephrite. And it's still intact, which is odd because so far none of the others have been."

"Give me that," she yelped, making a grab for the file. "Nephrite is another form of Jade!"

"And you think Evan could have used this as some, what?" Malcolm broke off for a second. "Some secret code system?" he questioned as he handed her file.

Jade nodded. "Maybe it's the envelope." She sat for a moment, her hand brushing the smooth surface of the folder. It didn't look worn and the label looked new. Unlike the hastily tossed and crumpled papers and folders still strewn across the floor.

Malcolm scooted closer and sat beside her as she opened the file and thumbed through the few sheets of carefully typed notes. "No envelope and no letter. So maybe somebody did go through it but kept it neat. Another taunt." Jade bit back her sigh. "The rest of this is all about researching the origins of the Khan." Disappointment bowed her shoulders. Why couldn't they catch one single break?

"Didn't you say he didn't want you to take on this commission? Maybe this will tell us why, because honestly, I don't believe in the curse. But the question of how the Queen got the Khan to give to Colonel Keller if the sapphire was guarded in a holy shrine is still a big question mark."

Jade turned back to page one, and together they carefully read each page. Nothing new was revealed in Evan's accounting of the history of the sapphire until they got to the bottom of the final page. She read it aloud 'I believe, due to the sanctity of the Khan to the people of the Steppe, and the fact that there are still guardians at the temple, this revered gem would never have been willingly given away. I also believe the curse is real, therefore dangerous, and will report my findings to Jade Laurent and David Cole. Mrs. Cole should not be allowed to buy this stone unless she plans on returning it to its rightful place.'

Jade closed the folder, then stared at Malcolm as they each processed Evan's report.

A crash of glass shattered the silence.

11

MALCOLM WAS UP IN A FLASH AND GRABBED HIS GUN FROM ITS holster. "Stay still," he whispered and left the room, but not before turning off the light.

The noise had seemed to come from the kitchen, and damn if dusk hadn't already fallen, so the subtle darkness would mask the intruder from being easily detected by the nosey Mrs. Smith.

Malcolm stood just inside the kitchen near the fridge, watching as a black-leather-gloved hand reached in, fumbled with the lock, and opened the door.

In seconds, Malcolm had his gun trained the intruder. "Down on your stomach, hands behind your back."

Apparently the threat was enough to have the man drop.

Malcolm bound his hands with zip cuffs, then helped him get to his feet.

He recognized him.

"Jade, it's safe. We're in the kitchen."

She came in and turned on the light. "David."

The utter disappointment in her voice scraped at Malcolm, but he dismissed the jealous emotion. This wasn't the time for anything but getting David Cole into the hands of the police.

Holstering the gun, he pulled his cell and hit 911. "Making a citizen's arrest for breaking and entering. Possible murder suspect. Back entrance. Off driveway." He rattled off the address.

"Murder suspect? What the hell are you talking about?" David yelled.

"Evan," Jade answered flatly.

"What?"

"And the theft of the Khan."

"No, you're completely wrong. Jade, you have it all wrong."

"Your mother didn't think so. She had one heart issue. Think of what this will do to her."

Malcolm heard the sirens. "You can tell it to your attorney. And you can stop struggling."

"I won't need to. I have proof on my phone." He shifted his shoulders back and forth as if trying to loosen the cuffs.

"Then your attorney will be happy." Malcolm didn't believe the man for a second.

"But it was stolen at the hospital—"

And that baloney just bore out his suspicion. "Convenient. You won't get out of those." Malcolm nodded to the plastic handcuffs. "So stop trying." David's glacial stare didn't faze him in the least.

"Jade, it's true. I thought Evan would have a copy of the transfer. That's why I'm here. I need it—"

"Yes, you do," Jade interrupted.

She got a pleading look. David was trying to soften her. Malcolm didn't think he'd have a chance in hell.

"Listen to me. I've driven past the house twice, and there have been no lights on either time. I had no idea where he was, so I figured this might be the only way to find the file he said he had."

"And your bike isn't as visible in darkness. Doesn't cut it,

Cole. You were here earlier. Your bike was seen. And the house is trashed. Why'd you come back?"

"My new motorcycle? I reported it stolen from the Denver office a month ago. I keep it to use when I'm in town. This time I had to rent a car."

"More convenient answers. We'll check on that once the PD gets here."

"What does the logo for your company look like?" Jade asked.

"What?"

"Just a rough sketch idea."

"A blue half globe made of dots—"

"That's all I needed. The bike had that logo on the tank. Why do all this destruction?" Jade waved her hand, encompassing the house.

"I didn't do anything."

David stopped twisting, which was better for him as the plastic cuffs were tight and rough. He stood straight, a bit less than Malcolm's six-plus feet. "Evan gave me the stone."

That even elicited a bark of disbelief from Jade. "David, come on. Nobody will believe that."

"His signature is on my phone."

"Phone again. Don't you have backup?"

Malcolm winced at the snark in her voice as David's eyes grew large.

"You may be a genius geek, but your story skills leave a lot to be desired."

"Police," a loud voice from outside the kitchen door announced.

"In here. Malcolm Talbot, PI, Jade Laurent, and in cuffs, David Cole."

Boulder's finest came in with weapons in hand. They saw

David's gloved hand with glass shards still embedded in the leather.

Malcolm showed them his PI license card. The first officer scanned it and then took phone numbers from him and Jade. Malcolm briefly recited the facts of the case and mentioned Denver PD detectives Tomba and Moore, to make sure Boulder PD knew other agencies were involved. The police marched David out of the house between them, this time with a set of police handcuffs securing his hands behind his back.

Then Malcolm and Jade were once again alone in the house.

Jade leaned against the sink. "Good thing Mrs. Smith apparently isn't home now, or she'd be over here in a flash." Harsh laughter erupted.

Malcolm saw her put a fist to her lips. "It's shock, Jade. It's okay to feel this. It's your body's way of releasing some tension."

"Oh my God." She pointed to the inside of the sink.

Malcolm turned to see what caused her exclamation. In the bottom, near the garbage disposal was a brown cigarette butt. "Evan didn't smoke, right? And David vapes?"

She nodded.

"See if you can find a plastic baggie. I'm going to find a spoon."

"Left of stove, second drawer," she directed.

Jade got the baggie out of a tall cupboard opposite the sink. Malcolm scooped up the butt and dumped it into the small bag.

"What does that mean?" she asked.

Malcolm leaned against the counter, folding his arms over his chest, buying a moment of time. Trying to figure out something that nagged at him.

"Malcolm?"

Time was up. "I don't know. Everything points to David. But it makes no sense. None of it. Omarr, your father, and now Evan? Why would David care about any of them?"

Jade winced and Malcolm kicked himself. "You know that's not what I meant. Let's get out of here."

He let her lead through the trashed living room, allowing her time if she wanted it. Knowing, too, that someday soon she'd have to come back and face all this. He didn't want her to have to do it alone. "I'll help with getting all this in order if you'd like. And we need to get that windowpane in the back door replaced."

Stopping mid step, she turned and leaned against him, her cheek pressed against his chest. "Honestly, that's the nicest thing you've ever said to me. But you're going to be way too busy to take time off to help. And I'll have to figure out his Tuscany property as well."

"I've always wanted to go to Italy. And Jade, despite what Tomba and Moore were insinuating about Evan's will, they're wrong. However, all that was his is yours now. No rush to do anything except the window. My offer will stand."

That earned him a brilliant smile.

MALCOLM MADE QUICK WORK OF GETTING THEM BACK TO THEIR borrowed digs, and Jade again mentally thanked Jason and Cate for loaning them this amazing house.

"Hey, food or nibbles?" she asked him from the kitchen. He'd gone to his room, not offering any explanation. Not that he needed one. But still it felt odd.

"Nibbles," he called out.

Scanning the fridge, she brought out a wedge of Brie, then found a box of crackers in the cupboard. "You get to pick the wine," she yelled.

"Okay," he said from right behind her.

"You move like a panther."

And received a grin.

Moments later they were sitting on the couch. Jade sat cross-legged so she could face Malcolm.

He poured the wine and Jade drank half of hers in one gulp.

"Whoa, go easy or else you'll fall asleep on the couch."

"I could do that. The nap earlier was great, but this evening …"

She watched as Malcolm took a long sip and she raised her brows. "Okay, so I can't drink like a fish, but you can?"

"Yep."

"Nope. What gives?"

"What do you mean?" he asked, spreading the softened Brie on a cracker.

"You're stalling. You have that look. I've seen it a dozen times in the past four days. You're thinking about something and trying to decide if you want to tell me."

He took a deep breath, and she steeled herself with another gulp of the wine, then refilled her glass.

"I keep circling back to the deaths of Omarr and your father and then the note found beside Evan's body."

"Yeah, that. I've been thinking about that … connection as well. It doesn't fit with the Khan and David. Why would he care if the circle was complete?"

"Exactly. But then we have Mrs. Cole's comment about David wouldn't, couldn't have. And he was at the airport when you called him about his mother's heart attack."

"Yes, so two conflicting thoughts. If he was at the airport, he was leaving, thus not after me, unless he was going to attempt it later, which we know now hasn't been the case. Nobody is dragging their feet on making the circle complete."

She took another fortifying sip of wine, then felt the warmth of his hand on her knee. Looking down, she felt as if his long, lean fingers, firm palm, and elegant wrist belonged right where they were. Felt that his heart was connected to this gesture. Not love, but maybe that close friendship she yearned for was something he also sought.

"Or."

She looked up from her study of his hand on her knee to see deep concern turning his blue eyes almost navy.

"Or he hired someone," he said gently. "We can't discount anything, Jade. It's possible he was lying and not at the airport at all. It'll be nearly impossible to get passenger manifests. But we can try. I'll see if Shelley can work her magic."

"I can't believe Evan gave the Khan to him. He would never betray me like that. Yet from what we uncovered today, Evan felt the stone needed to go back to the original owners. And it would make sense as Evan's prosthetic compartment wasn't damaged but had been opened properly by him. All that would mean a complete circle there. And worse, for some reason his mother seemed to think it was David who could have done this. And he has the Khan. It still all points to David."

"But, Jade, since Evan believed in the curse—"

"Which is why I now know the reason for his being so adamant about taking on the courier job himself. He was protecting me."

"Maybe David believes the curse as well. And he was protecting his mother. So just think about this for a minute. Evan did want to talk to David about the stone, the idea that it should be returned to its rightful place. But being Evan, he first had to get the job finished, and David didn't want his mother to have the gem in her possession for even a second. Love can lead to all sorts of rash or inexplicable actions."

Jade wondered for a split second if he was also thinking about his father's behavior, simply deciding life was over when his wife died.

"We need to find Evan's phone as well. I'll start the team on tracing his."

"I didn't think about it being missing, but it wasn't found with him, was it? I honestly can't recall."

"No, it wasn't."

"Do you suppose that's why David was so startled when I mentioned a phone backup? That it would have incriminating information, not the clear-his-name info he stated?" She let loose a deep sigh. "My head hurts from all this thinking."

Malcolm laughed. "You know, you're quite good at this, looking at all the angles, spit-balling ideas."

Jade opened her mouth, then shut it immediately.

"To paraphrase you, what?"

"Later. It has nothing to do with all this at hand." She braved his stare. She wasn't willing to talk about her thoughts for a new direction for her life. In fact, it seemed too radical to really contemplate, yet it pulled at her. "I did have an idea about the only intact folder at Evan's."

"Okay, I get the subject change. Tell me when you're ready. What's your idea?"

"Why only that folder? I think it was left intact to throw us off the scent of David. I mean he came back to the scene as well. It all seems so planned out. Like a scene in a movie or a book. Calculated to throw off suspicion."

12

Sunday used to be the day Jade baked, read, and relaxed. It was something her father did and insisted she do as well. No work, no phone calls from clients. Even the ones that had his private number knew better than to call on a Sunday.

Not this Sunday. After too much wine last night, a reaction to the events of the day, David's arrest, and facing the wanton destruction of Evan's home, Jade woke up early after a fitful sleep. Hoping the day would be a continuation of the springlike weather, she pushed the button by the bed that lifted the window shades. Her wish was granted, and Jade delighted in watching the dawn paint the sky with the teals, rusts, and grays that Claude Monet used in his *Impression, Sunrise*.

Her lips turned upward in a small smile at her fanciful thoughts. And the fact that she was looking forward to seeing Megan. She missed her closest buddy.

Dressed, with minimal makeup dashed on, she entered the great room of their borrowed digs in time to hear Malcolm wrap up a call. "Great news, keep me posted."

Jade poured a cup of coffee from the French press and

waited impatiently for him to turn around and share the "great news."

"Mike's nephew was returned. He was basically left at the front door of the family home just before sunrise—"

"Is he okay? Malcolm, tell me he's okay."

"Yeah, mostly. He remembers nothing except a prick on his neck. Mike found a puncture wound we think was made by a dart. He's kind of sick to his stomach and was blindfolded the entire time. The only sound he heard was engine noise, no voices. Apparently he thinks the vehicle stopped for a while, but he can't really remember. He thinks it was a van with an odd smell. But since he was drugged, we can't be sure of any of his senses working fully."

"The poor guy. And his family? Mike?"

"Okay, so they say. Mike sounded fine, but I get the sense we'll need a chat later."

She looked at Malcolm over the rim of her cup. "Are you blaming yourself?"

"No—Yes." He shook his head as if to clear it. "But right now, we need to pick up Megan and head to your office before Boulder wakes up."

"Little do you know. There are runners, dog walkers, and hikers already out and about."

"Then drink up and let's roll. If you still want to do this."

"'No—Yes,' to quote you."

"You don't have to go—"

"Yes, I do. Laurent Art Brokers is still in business, and I've got to run it. I need the information on current contracts. Which jobs have to be seriously looked at and action taken because of auction deadlines, or those where the purchase needs completion. Then we can decide what we can put on the back burner for a while."

"Then let's roll."

They used Marta's BMW as a decoy again. Jade knew that as the crow flies, Greg and Megan's cabin was less than a mile away, over a canyon and up to Kinnikinic Road at the top of the cul-de-sac.

However, it shouldn't have surprised her that Malcolm took a circuitous route, checking behind them the entire time. Ten minutes later, as they entered the park, Jade noticed he dialed Megan and told her they were a minute away, and that he was driving a black BMW.

Sure enough, just as they slowed to a stop, Meg popped out of the house and keyed something into her cell phone, probably an alarm code. She waved the phone at Malcolm as she ran to the car and jumped in the back seat.

Jade leaned over the console and awkwardly hugged her. "I've missed you."

"Me too, buddy o'mine. Me too."

"What? Did you guys compare notes to dress alike?" Malcolm asked as he pulled away.

Jade looked down at her black leggings and black printed tunic, then glanced back at Megan to find her buddy wore nearly the same thing. They grinned.

"It's all that time working together—we're nearly sisters," Megan said with a wink, looking straight into the rearview mirror.

Jade knew Malcolm got the look. Suddenly it felt very much like one big family outing, though it was anything but. Nevertheless, she hugged the feeling to her heart.

Megan didn't bring up Evan, and Jade decided she wouldn't bring up David Cole until they were in the office. She knew her friend wanted answers.

Malcolm pulled into the parking lot of her building. Instantly he braked hard and Jade instinctively put a hand on the dash to brace herself.

"I don't believe it!"

Jade looked up at Malcolm's growl. "What?" She followed his stare.

Straight in front of them, taunting them, was the red Ducati bike. The rider was dressed in black, helmet on.

Her world narrowed to the figure in front of them.

Jade tried hard to imprint a sense of the rider's body build into her brain for later use. But nothing would stick. Just the horrible, slow-motion sensation of time decelerating and whatever bit of security she'd felt with David's arrest disappearing at the sight of the rider facing them as if in a duel.

To the death.

He gave them that arrogant two-fingered salute and gunned the bike, doing a wheelie, barely clearing their vehicle as he shot out of the lot.

As Jade turned, open-mouthed, to follow the black figure with her gaze, Megan asked from the back seat, "Who's that?"

Before Jade could answer, the earth swelled and rolled, rocking the heavy SUV. She twisted back in her seat and in the same instant she saw the windows of her building blow, deadly shards of glass arrowing out and downward.

The very air around them crackled with an ominous energy.

Then paper and debris floated down as great black puffs of smoke billowed from the gaping wound in her building.

Her instinct pushed her to run for her building to protect it, and she was halfway out of the BMW before she felt Malcolm's hand clamp on her left arm, stopping her. Only then did she realize her lungs begged for air, and she breathed.

"Close the door, *now*."

Looking at Malcolm and his abrupt nod at her, she understood just how close she'd come to personal disaster, fueled by adrenaline fury. She slammed the door closed as

Malcolm reversed the BMW out of the driveway and out of harm's way. He stopped at the curb and let the vehicle idle.

"How the hell does he know our movements? We didn't find a beacon in your purse or on your phone."

"Wait. What? Malcolm, you mean this nut job is one step ahead of you?" Megan's voice rose to a squeak. "And he wasn't out to kill you just now? He was sending a message?"

Jade turned and held out her trembling hand to Megan, who clasped it tightly. "Oh, I think that's still his plan. But first he's out to destroy everything, then me, us—"

"*Us*? What haven't you told me?"

"He's been in my house, Meg. But there is so much more—" A sound pierced the ringing in her ears caused by the blast, and Jade turned in her seat, concentrating on the wail. "Listen."

"I hear sirens," Megan said. "As it should be."

"No, they're coming too quickly, Meg," Jade said.

"Huh? What are you talking about? They should be coming now."

"I hear them too. He tipped them off. That's the only way," Malcolm agreed flatly.

Jade's fear level was high, beyond calculation, but along with it rose a red fury. And with the fury came a deadly energy and a calm that was icy in its preciseness.

Red lights flashing and siren wailing, a Boulder police car pulled to the curb, followed closely by two firetrucks and an ambulance veering into the parking lot of her—she shook her head—*destroyed* office building.

She grabbed the door handle, ready to leave the vehicle again, but Malcolm put a warning hand on her thigh.

"Let them come to us, and everyone be still. No fast movements."

Officer Arnold, the officer she'd met—was it only yesterday

at Evan's house?—approached from the rear, weapon at the ready.

Malcolm rolled down the window on his side. "Malcolm Talbot, Jade Laurent, and Megan Rice in the vehicle, Officer Arnold. This is Ms. Laurent's office building."

"Jeeze, Talbot, you're like a bad penny."

OFFICER ARNOLD BENT TO LOOK INTO THE SUV. "THOUGHTS ON who did this?" the red-haired officer said, then turned away to cough and fan the smoke-filled air.

Malcolm opened his mouth—

"David Cole. But how while he's in custody?" Jade leaned over Malcolm as she interrupted him. He could feel her white-hot anger vibrating through her jacket.

"Which I'm assuming he still is?" Malcolm added.

"Oh, yeah. He'd not going anywhere, even after he's arraigned. Murder? He ain't gonna get bail."

"Malc, Jade? Look behind you," Megan interrupted. "The last thing Laurent Art Brokers needs right now is the press."

A KBCF news van was pulling to the curb at the other side of the building's parking lot entrance. Malcolm bit back his groan. "Can we do this later, Arnold?" And nodded over his shoulder toward the van.

"You know where to find me."

Malcolm watched as the officer walked back to his cruiser, apparently ignoring the questions already being called to him by the reporter getting out of the van.

And this particular reporter was the last person Malcolm wanted near Jade. Or himself, at the moment. Making a swift decision, he decided it was best to confront her instead of being ambushed. "Listen up, both of you. Deidre Allen is the reporter.

She's good, very good. I'm going to head her off but expect her to come and try and interview you. Say nothing and remember, the camera will pick up every facial expression. Got it?"

Megan nodded.

Malcolm waited impatiently for Jade's agreement.

She shook her head. "I have a sense he'll be watching. I want him to know I'm not broken. Will *not* be broken."

"I think he knows that already. You were here. You are showing you're strong. He doesn't like it."

"But I'm okay with talking to her."

"I'm not." With that, he got out of the BMW and approached the svelte blonde. They had a past, and he'd found her to be a witty and entertaining woman beneath her tough reporter persona. Right now, he didn't know which Deidre he was going to get, but he'd bet on the tough-as-nails side of her.

He positioned himself between her and the BMW, hoping he could forestall her long enough—*for what? The cavalry wasn't coming.*

"Malcolm, good to see you, I think. It means you're either on a case or you were going to have breakfast on the Mall," Deidre joked.

"Can you do this later?"

"Not really. Got something to hide?"

"No, but my client has been through enough right now."

Deidre studied her phone for a moment. "Jade Laurent is your client? I recall her father was killed in a hit and run last year."

"How did you know her name?"

"The tip that was called in to the station said to be prepared and gave her name and the address of the building."

"Ready, Deidre," her crew called.

He watched as she slipped into reporter mode.

"Breaking news. Deidre Allan, live at the scene of an

explosion near the Pearl Street Mall, an office building belonging to Jade Laurent. First responders are on the scene, and so far, thankfully, it seems the building was empty."

Deidre dodged around him to the right, heading for the vehicle he'd just gotten out of. Her camera man was following, telltale red light still glowing. They stopped at the front of the BMW with the camera pointed right at the windshield.

There was no way Jade could avoid being caught on camera. Unless she ducked, which he knew she wouldn't do.

"Ms. Laurent, any thought on how this happened? We got a tip that it was a bombing," Deidre yelled.

Annoyed that the reporter had completely ignored his reasonable request, he realized that while Deidre might have been a fun date, Jade was the one he cared about and wanted to explore a relationship with once this was over.

Momentarily stunned by that realization, he started to say something that would take the heat off Jade. Then he stopped. Anything he said would be caught by the same camera's recorder and possibly complicate everything. *As if it's not complicated on so many levels now. This case isn't making sense, and you're involved with your client. Two negative factors for any investigation.*

He got swiftly into the SUV, backed up and squealed around Deidre and her camera man, with just enough clearance to express his don't-ever-call-me-again meaning.

Checking the rearview mirror, he didn't see anyone following, including the KBCF truck. He took a moment to glance at Jade. Her hands were clenched in her lap. Megan was leaning forward, hand on her friend's shoulder in support.

"Meg, I'm taking you home. Do what you've been doing for security. Greg will be home today."

"Malcolm, he's coming home day after tomorrow, remember?"

Malcolm didn't bother to correct her. He punched a code into this phone and Greg answered immediately. Malcolm put the phone in speaker mode. "Listen, buddy, you got more than enough info on your case. Forget the commercial flight, charter a plane. I need your skills. Now."

"Megan?" Greg asked.

Malcolm jerked his head toward Megan to indicate she could answer that one.

"I'm fine. But this case with Jade—"

"What case? Is she okay?"

"She's okay. But somehow a bastard is one step ahead of us, and we've gotta know before he makes good on his threat—"

"She's in danger," Greg said flatly.

"Yeah, like someone wants her dead."

"Holy—Got it, see you soon." And the line went dead.

Malcolm pulled in front of Meg and Greg's cabin and let the SUV idle.

Meg leaned over the console and gave Jade a kiss on the cheek. "I'm sorry to be so blunt, but I wanted Greg to know the unvarnished truth. If Malcolm wants him here it's a big deal."

Then Malcolm got his kiss. "Meg—"

"No worries. I'll text you when I'm inside and the cabin's armed."

Malcolm scanned the area as Megan hustled to the door and slipped inside. His phone rang and he glanced down. "She's in. Let's go."

Jade turned in her seat to look back at the little cabin. "I'm glad Greg is coming back. I'll feel that Megan is safer with him there."

"I have a feeling he'll be more in his lab than the cabin, but knowing another level of protection is in place is good."

"Malcolm." She grabbed his arm, and he slammed on the

brakes. "I've got to let Aksel know. This idiot knows too much. I've got to warn him."

"Call him. You've got his number, right?"

Malcolm drove as Jade dialed, then put the call on speakerphone.

"Aksel?"

"Jade? What's wrong?"

"You have to be extremely cautious. Stay in the house. Evan's house was broken into and trashed. And now—"

"Jade?"

"The office has been destroyed. Bombed."

"*Chérie*, are you okay? I can come by. The place where I'm staying is up the canyon, but I can drive it fast."

Jade glanced at Malcolm to see if he had any input, but he made no gesture. It was her decision and Aksel was her only family left.

Not true, you have your ohana family, of which you are a part.

"No. I want you to stay put and safe. I've got Malcolm." And she realized she meant it.

Feeling Malcolm's gaze, she turned to meet it, seeing his lips lift in the slightest of smiles.

"Yes. Yes, you do," Aksel finally replied.

13

BACK IN THEIR BORROWED SAFE HOUSE, JADE HEADED TO HER bedroom, telling Malcolm she'd be back in a few minutes. He didn't stop her.

Alone in the great room, staring out the windows to the north, Malcolm pondered Jade's words. *I've got Malcolm.*

Those three words were loaded with promise, and he forced himself to admit it, fear.

Fear that he couldn't keep her safe. That he'd been compromised by his emotions over her from the get-go. He was a PI, not a bodyguard.

Fear that he was putting too much emotion into those words. That they were ohana, not friends. And fear that he wanted so much more than simply being friends.

His usually clear-headed, true-north compass was off, and he knew the best thing was going back to being client and PI.

Malcolm just didn't know how to do it and not tear apart Jade's fragile world any more than it already had been. She trusted him.

But he needed to do this. If David had such deep pockets that he could hire a squad of goons and somehow had technology that was beyond their capability to recognize, then Jade had to be kept in a locked house. No more going out. No more anything.

Have this nightmare of a case be over and then see if he could rebuild whatever had started between them.

He looked toward the bedroom he knew was hers and found the woman who had somehow burrowed her way into his heart walking toward him.

"Malcolm. We need to talk."

Maybe she was going to make it easy for him. Which didn't stop the bleakness that began to fill his soul.

They headed to the couch they'd sat on last night. No wine, no nibbles. Nothing to break the harshness of a difficult face-to-face conversation.

"I'm furious. I want to scream and pound. I want David in prison. But I also want you to stop feeling like you've failed," Jade said quietly.

He opened his mouth only to see her hand rise.

"I thought I could help. But instead I nearly got us all killed. Granted, whoever was on the bike—I'm assuming someone David hired—stopped us before we got too close. But had we been ten or fifteen feet closer to the building, those shards of glass and shattered brick could have rained down *on* us. The SUV wouldn't have protected us.

"I know this was staged to take the very last things I cared about away from me. But I also realized you and Megan are people I very much care for. So, I accept that I might be too late with this, but I will do whatever you say I should do. I can't risk putting you in danger. And I think as furious as I am, I'm even more scared."

"That's my fault—"

"This isn't about fault. And anyway, you're wrong. This is about facing up to the fact that I can't live under a cloud, waiting for him to strike. You need to find all that you can to put the bastard away for life, and you don't need me to get in the way."

All he could do was nod. She was right. He'd admitted it to himself moments ago. So he should feel a bit of relief. The question was, where to move her? Or should he keep her here? Gus and Jason had top-of-the-line security, yet somehow David was ahead of them.

But now that he was in jail, it was possible his connection with his henchmen was broken. The bombing could have been his last command. And since he didn't seem to be averse to killing, Malcolm was sure David would have been Jade's assassin —had he not been in custody.

It broke him to see her head bowed, her spirit wounded. "Come here."

After a moment's hesitation, she scooted over, close enough that he could touch her. "You are brave, a fighter, and I want you to know this is not giving up. We're still going to find enough information to nail David for this. And Greg will be here soon to help—"

Jade's cell phone rang, interrupting him. She turned it off. It rang twice more and finally she looked at the number. "Smythe. I'll call him back. It's work, and it's not going to matter right now anyway. He'll have to find a new broker to handle his commissions."

"Talk to him if you want to. I'm not going anywhere."

And for an instant the gratitude in her gaze gut-punched him. Was she grateful that she could take the call, or that he wasn't going anywhere?

She remembered to put the phone in speaker mode.

"Jade, thank God you picked up. Are you okay? I'm at the freight counter at the airport, and they had the news on in the waiting room. A bomb?"

Malcolm blinked, wondering that she didn't grimace at each

shrill word. That man's voice was torture on the ears. And after her reaction to that first high-pitched sentence, he had his answer. The gratitude that reflected in her eyes was for Malcolm Talbot, PI.

"Yes, a bomb. It pretty much took out the building."

"Then I'm coming back."

"No, Smythe. Take the painting to Hawaii. The best thing you can do is deliver it and make the customer happy."

"But—"

"We'll talk when you get home. I've got lots to think about and I need time, okay?"

"Okay. I guess."

Jade disconnected the call and put the phone on the coffee table.

"Who is Smythe? And what a voice."

She cracked a small smile. "He's one of the best reproduction artists in the country. And yes, he sounds whiny."

Shifting on the couch so she was closer, Jade leaned against him. "Is it okay, just for a moment?"

"Sure. Stay there as long as you want." His arm went around her, and he idly rubbed her shoulders, feeling the tension knot. Working his fingers into the muscle, he felt her wince, and lifted his hands off her shoulder.

"Don't stop it—hurts so good."

"You're a mass of tight muscles. Turn around."

She did, but she didn't move far away.

He dug in, feeling the knots loosen, and heard her sigh.

"The day is only half over, but I feel like twenty-fours of horror have been compressed into it. I wasn't kidding when I said I had a lot to think about."

"Maybe just let it rest. Thinking that hard after so much emotion usually creates the wrong answer."

"When is Greg coming?"

"He should be landing at Front Range soon. It's not a long flight."

"Megan worries about him and his job."

"I think it's time he and I discuss taking him off 'active duty.' He's a gadget guy. That's his love, and if the Kahuna Group idea flies, he'll be happiest doing what he loves."

"And you?"

"The group won't break up Harrison & Talbot, it will just broaden our horizons. I like to investigate, as I said, and put the puzzle pieces together. If we expand our possibilities for clients, we'll need to hire more staff."

Jade turned in his arms and touched his cheek. He knew something was brewing in the back of her mind, but more, her trust, the intimacy of her gesture, allowed him to focus now on her lips.

Taking that kiss that was forbidden. He was bound by his code of honor. He'd already tiptoed past that code in the way he allowed her to be close and, more importantly, the way he *wanted* her to be close.

He'd make sure they got the chance to explore this once the case was solved and Jade was out from under this death threat. He had the sense they were close to solving the case.

Her eyes fluttered closed and she leaned deeper into his arms. He let her sleep as his mind ticked off all the incidents.

It had to be David. Now they just had to find the evidence to prove it. And Malcolm was good at that.

14

JADE STIRRED, REALIZING SHE WAS STILL SNUGGLED IN MALCOLM'S embrace. She had no idea how long she'd been in his arms on the couch or what woke her until she heard his phone. "I'm beginning to rekindle my dislike of those," she muttered as she stretched. Then she moved so Malcolm could reach the offending, noise-making phone on the table.

Had he dozed as well? Had she imagined that she felt him kiss the top of her head and heard his whispered "Rest, petite warrior"?

Malcolm as usual, didn't bother to look at the phone's screen. He knew the ringtone and just pushed the button for the speaker. "Shel, what's up."

"Is Ms. Laurent with you, boss?"

"Yep, got you on speaker phone."

"I got some news from Jana."

"Jana?" Jade asked.

"Shelley's source at the FBI," Malcolm answered.

"FBI?"

"I asked Shelley to see if she could find out why the only information I could dig up on your trio of business founders was just the basics. Usually I can go deep, financials, businesses, employment, back to school grades. There was nothing there prior to their coming to the States. Not for your father, Omarr Basarias, or even much on Evan Fischer."

That didn't make any sense. Her father and Omarr had owned a gallery together. Evan was American and should be in the system, even if her father and Omarr were French and wouldn't have much history prior to the American gallery opening. For taxes if nothing else. She'd been naturalized long ago and held dual citizenship. There should have been something there. "Shelley, any information you have, I want," Jade said.

She met Malcolm's glance and saw admiration. Jade wasn't sure she earned it, but this material could hold a vital missing part to the puzzle. And both her life and Aksel's may well depend on it.

"Hello, Ms. Laurent. Jana, an old college buddy, who as Malcolm says is my contact in the FBI, finally got back to me. She said the data was buried pretty deep ... in covert ops, but it wasn't classified, thank goodness. Evan Fischer initially worked at the FBI in the money-laundering division. Later he was recruited to work domestically, then internationally with Interpol to uncover art forgers. He pulled in Gerard Laurent and Omarr Basarias to work with him."

Jade couldn't stifle her gasp.

"You had no idea?" Malcolm asked.

She shook her head, utterly bewildered.

"Jana, any idea why Laurent and Basarias were recruited?" Malcolm asked.

"Yep. Are you sure you want me to go on, Ms. Laurent?"

"Yes, of course." Jade welcomed Malcolm pulling her back against him, feeling safe within his arms. Jana's question sounded ominous.

"This apparently happened after they were charged with art fraud. Mr. Fischer was able to convince Interpol, who had been working with the FBI, that they would be an asset to the group. It was that or spending time in a French prison. Who better to catch a forger than a forger?"

Who better to catch a forger than a forger? Confusion swamped any rational thought. Jade pushed away from Malcolm, launching off the couch. Embarrassment warred with anger. She marched to the kitchen island, then back to the couch. Then she did the circuit again until she stood in front of the coffee table, facing Malcolm, hands on her hips. "I don't understand this at all. How could they have kept this from me? They lived a lie. I've been living their lie."

It took all her effort to not pick up the wine bottle and hurl it at the fireplace. Had it been her house, she might have done just that, aiming at that farce of a framed picture on her mantel. Family? Ha. They lied to her.

When Malcolm moved the bottle out of her reach, she gave him a humpf.

"They didn't lie to you, honey, they simply didn't tell you. After all it was *their* past. If you've lived long enough, you have something in your past you're not proud of. The idea is to move on, to be better, to let it be a lesson."

He patted the spot on the couch she'd vacated. "Are you up to checking what you know against what I have here?" He held up the phone. "Shelley forwarded me the info she got from Jana. Okay?"

Jade sat, but all the way at the end of the comfortable couch, resting against the arms. She nodded for him to start.

He swiveled to face her. "You were ten when you arrived in Denver?"

She nodded. "Is that on your phone?"

He pointed to his head. "Nope, from our conversation a few days ago when you were telling me about the picture."

"Ah, the picture." She humpfed again. "Yes, ten."

"Omarr and your dad opened the second gallery at that time in Denver."

"Yes, with Evan. Although he was never a partner. I always thought he didn't much like the business end. Then Dad decided he'd had enough and opened the art brokerage. Apparently Omarr bought him out, but they still shared a customer base. Omarr changed the name of both galleries to Basarias et Fils at the time. Aksel was managing the gallery in Paris then. Thus the 'Fils' for son."

"You were in your teens when the art brokerage opened?"

She nodded. "And we moved to Boulder. I went to Boulder High and then, as you know, to the École Des Beaux-Arts. After returning to the States, I got a degree from the Gemological Institute of America."

Jade rested her elbow on her thigh and her chin in her palm. "This all makes much more sense now. Evan taught a section of art history classes at the Beaux-Arts that somehow turned into the methodology for forgery. Even Aksel took that class when he was a student there. It was almost a requirement.

"And while Evan was there for the duration of his teaching stint each year, he'd take me to various galleries and have me inspect paintings. I never questioned how we could get into those back rooms or have the vaults opened to us. I just thought it was because of his stature at the school. There were amazing forgeries and reproductions. Some were easier to spot than others. Now there are expensive, high-tech methods for looking deep into the layers of the paintings. But the eye is the first tool."

She trailed off. So much made sense now. Then a horrible thought struck her. "All this information can never come to light.

It'll ruin the gallery's reputation, and all our clients will wonder about the authenticity of their work."

"Jade, it doesn't need to. This was long, long ago. They went straight and actually helped unmask forgers."

With Malcolm's comment, her stubborn flicker of an idea seemed absolutely the right course for her to take. And as that idea comforted her a bit, a forger's daughter out to unmask forgers, she thought of Aksel. "I wonder if Aksel knows?"

"Do you want to tell him?"

"I guess I should, but not tonight, maybe not tomorrow. When this nightmare is over. Maybe."

"Speaking of Aksel, his mother, Heloise, who—"

"Yeah," Jade interrupted and kept her gaze glued to his face. She saw his jaw tighten, knowing that he and Aksel shared a tragedy. Heloise died in childbirth. "If you've read the histories then you know Aksel never had the joy of knowing his mother. He was less than a year old when she died." Jade pointed to his phone. "You also know that Omarr never remarried. Heloise was his life, his love. I always sensed a deep wound—"

And she saw the wound reflected in Malcolm's gaze. His father had carried a similar wound, yet his reaction had been the opposite of Omarr's, who went forward with his life.

Malcolm glanced down and started scrolling on the phone, yet she still felt the connection with him. Perhaps opening up as he'd done with her had brought them closer.

Perhaps this was a good thing.

He looked up again, "There's no mention of your mother."

Jade wrinkled her brow into a frown. She'd been the one to ask that nothing be hidden. She wanted everything out in the open, yet she'd never confided to another soul how she felt about being abandoned. Not to Megan. Not even her father had been privy to her fears. God knows he hadn't needed any more suffering over the false heart of the only woman he ever loved.

Suddenly the words poured from Jade's heart. "I guess I was about five, and as you know, we were living in France. I never really knew Mère ... she and Papa never married. But I could always tell when she was there for a visit because I could smell her rose perfume long before I ever saw her."

Jade's thoughts flew back in time and she remembered the bold and vibrant colors of their apartment, yet the memories of her mother always remained veiled in gray melancholy. "Mère would peck Papa on the cheek when she came to him from"—she shrugged—"wherever she'd been. She always had a lot of makeup on and dressed very chicly in flowing robes that looked exotic to me. I think now she was a dancer at the Moulin Rouge."

Realizing she'd clasped her hands so tightly that they hurt, Jade relaxed her fingers. "One day Papa brought home a beautiful dress of green as a present for me. He said the color matched my eyes, and it did. It was made of the softest velvet, with a bow of black satin low on the waist. I adored it and couldn't wait for Mère to see it on me."

She smiled in sad remembrance. "He'd get so excited when Mère stayed with us. He even had an expensive housekeeper come clean the flat and prepare all sorts of delicious meals he could reheat when they grew hungry. I ate whenever I wanted. I guess he kind of forgot about me when she was around. It didn't matter, I could go play and then eat when I wanted, or even go and see Omarr and Aksel. They seemed to know when Mère was around."

Sitting still proved impossible with the turmoil swirling inside her. Jade got up and paced in front of the couch. "One afternoon, knowing Mère was coming, I kept impatiently peeking around the corner of my bedroom door barely able to contain my excitement. Once Papa had seated Mère in her favorite chair in the sunroom at the rear of the apartment and poured her a glass of wine, I ran in with my new green dress on.

"The sun turned Mère's hair to a fiery color. I wandered over, fascinated, and reached out to pat it. She swatted my hand away and told me never to touch her without first asking permission. That I might muss her." Jade couldn't keep the bitterness from her voice.

"She then turned to Papa and asked him why he picked that horrible color of green for that silly little dress. I started to cry. Papa picked me up and tried to stop my tears. Mère got angrier and angrier, screeching at him to shut me up. Papa pleaded with me to hush, and finally I understood that I must do what he asked to make him happy. For if Mère was happy, he was happy."

Jade knew her words had tumbled over themselves, keeping tempo with the increased steps of her pacing. She stopped to look at Malcolm. She tried to read his eyes but couldn't decipher his feelings. "Do you want to hear more?"

He nodded.

"I fell asleep on the red velvet settee, tired I guess, from all my tears. When I woke up, Mère and Papa were having a terrible fight. I lay still as possible.

"He asked Mère to come to the States with him and me. She laughed like a crazy woman. It scared me. She told him she'd never wanted to be saddled with a husband, let alone a brat of a child," Jade whispered. "She said there was no way she'd give up her lifestyle to accommodate him. That he was a convenience. Papa begged her, kneeling at her chair. Finally, she said she would reconsider staying with him if he forgot about going to America, and only if he got rid of … me."

Jade moved to the large French doors and watched the stars emerge as dusk fell. As if nature were telling her that it was indeed the right time to let go of this vivid memory. She turned back to Malcolm.

"The room was suddenly quiet and then Papa jumped up, his face purple, and I saw Mère cower in her chair. He didn't strike her, but I whimpered, terrified. I'd never seen him angry like that. Without a word, he picked me up and we left the apartment, without even coats. We went back the next morning. I never saw Mère again, but I knew even at that age I'd always do whatever my father asked of me. He'd chosen me over her.

"Five years later we made the trip to America. Dad asked me to call him Dad instead of Papa when we got to the States, like he wanted that part of his life erased."

"Your dad really loved you," Malcolm stated softly.

"Yes, he did." She felt Malcolm's warmth and knew he stood close behind her.

"You don't know how lucky you were to have that love in your life." Malcolm's arms wrapped around her, pulling her back to rest against him.

His heartbeat echoing hers, Jade leaned onto the hardness of his body and allowed herself to bask in his understanding, to soak up his strength. Allowed herself a few more moments of pretending that this is what a couple did. They bolstered and encouraged each other. They didn't demand and threaten.

That love enhanced a couple, didn't warp them.

That true love didn't demand but gave.

That love didn't wrap you in a cocoon as protection, but let you run and breathe and make mistakes and then picked you up and dusted you off.

But that was for other people. Not Jade Laurent. She might be shedding those swaddling clothes, but she bet she'd never be fully free.

∽

MALCOLM TURNED JADE IN HIS ARMS AND BENT HIS HEAD SLOWLY, knowing this move was foolish and not caring. Jade had opened her soul to him, and there was nothing he wanted more than this kiss.

He moved slowly, giving her the time to back away, to tell him she didn't think the same way he did.

She didn't move.

Cupping her cheeks, he put every ounce of understanding into his expression, telling her that what she'd just done was powerful and that he'd treat her confidence as a precious gift.

She closed her eyes, her lips slightly apart as if in anticipation. Or invitation.

He bent closer and tasted her, his touch soft, still uncertain if she wanted this. Until she reached up and pulled his head closer.

He felt as if he'd come home. That their hearts were melded.

He kept the fire the kiss ignited to a gentle burn as he ran his hands lightly up and down her back, feeling the planes of her shoulder blades, the slim column of her neck. And the pressure of her body against his.

The light feathery touches she gave him were a form of agony. To take this further was insanity.

This was for later, to explore and learn each other.

With utmost slowness, he broke their kiss and rested his chin on the top of her head. Jade's rapid breathing matched his own. Thankfully, she didn't pull away. There was no regret in this kiss. Unless the fact that it shouldn't have happened at all was the core quandary.

"Don't regret this, Malcolm Talbot. I don't, not for a minute." Jade raised her head. He read the truthfulness in her words.

"Neither do I."

She reached up to cup his cheek. "Where this will lead is a

question we can answer later, but now, I think my pendant clasp is caught on my shirt label."

He chuckled. "Nice segue. Turn around and I'll see if I can untangle it."

Moments later the stunning pendant was in his hand. And a sudden horrifying thought cascaded through his brain.

"How long have you had this?"

"Since I turned eighteen. I never take it off. Well, almost never—"

Her eyes grew large at the same time Malcolm's phone rang with Greg's tone. He disarmed and unlocked the door so his partner could enter.

15

JADE, WITH MALCOLM BESIDE HER, SAT ACROSS FROM GREG AT THE kitchen counter, watching as he turned the pendant over in his hands.

"Okay," he said, holding it up to study it in the light. "Go through each part again so I can understand it."

"The metal is platinum. The imperial jade is held in place with a bezel and the pendant has a filigree backing, but it's now hidden. The red stones are ruby cabochons again set with a bezel. My father gave me the pendant on my eighteenth birthday. It was made around the time of Louis the Sixteenth's reign in France. They started using platinum as a jewelry metal more widely about that time.

"About two years ago, before Omarr's death"—she glanced at Malcolm, knowing he was putting together a timeline in his mind—"the filigree backing was becoming thin and unstable. I didn't want a solid back put on as it ruins the heritage of the piece. But there really wasn't another choice. Dad sent it back to Paris with my instructions on what I wanted—in fact I sketched a backing that would slide onto the original mounting. Aksel brought it back with him while on a visit to the Denver gallery. In fact, he clasped it around my neck."

Jade bowed her head. "I feel so stupid. We looked through my phone and my purse."

"Jade, that repair happened before David."

"Yes, but ... remember how it just got entangled in my shirt label? It happened once before, and David had to unclasp it to get it untangled. You would have thought I'd realize it was gone —after all, I wear it all the time, but I didn't realize he'd slipped it into his pocket. Maybe that's when he added the tracker. He returned it the next day. He said so it gave him an excuse to see me again."

"Maybe you were distracted by David."

She met Malcolm's bland glance. "It was just a kiss," she said softly, putting as much sincerity as possible in those words, wanting him to know that what she'd shared with him was so much more than 'just a kiss.' "But Omarr and my father had nothing to do with the Khan or David. I'm more confused than ever."

"The circle the first note referred to could still be the Khan's heritage. Thus, David's involvement. Your father's death may have been an accident, and Omarr's truly health related. Or the Khan had nothing to do with it, and it's a vendetta of some sort. And as I said, the extra person mentioned in the note on your mirror could be Aksel," Malcolm said.

Malcolm's explanation was short and concise and complete up to this moment.

Hearing the report as simple bullet-pointed facts, it sounded unbelievable that this was actually happening. That the family lineage of Laurent, Basarais, and even Fischer, though he had no children, would be wiped out. Fini.

"What the hell have you uncovered, Talbot?" Greg asked.

"Can we take the back off?"

Jade was grateful that Greg focused back on the matter at hand as he kept gently turning the pendant over in his hands. "Not without tools. See the tiny notch? That can be pried up carefully with a jeweler's screwdriver, and the new back part removed so the pendant can be pulled out."

"Greg, is it possible for a receiver or GPS to be crafted into something this small?" Malcolm asked.

"Sure. I've never heard of anything smaller than a quarter, which this would have to be to fit inside the back, but you know how fast technology changes," Greg said.

"And through metal?"

"Sure, depending on the metal. Jade, I think the best bet is for me to take this to the office lab. I'll treat it as carefully as I can."

"If the pendant has been the conduit, then I never want to see it again."

"I think it's highly likely that's what has been keeping David on track. But remember, he's in custody now. And even though I'm sure he lied about his phone being stolen, he can't make contact with the tracker. And with Greg taking it, it's no longer tracking us, Jade."

"It makes sense." Jade nodded to Malcolm. "But as it's still working, it'll track Greg."

"Only for a short while, and again, David doesn't have any access to direct the activities of his minions. I don't know if we're going down a rabbit hole. But we need to know if that," Malcolm pointed to the pendant in Greg's palm, "plays any part in this whole messed-up scenario."

Greg wrapped the pendant in a paper napkin, pocketed it, and got off his stool. "Nice of Jason to loan you his digs, or should I say Marta's." Greg whistled as he looked around.

"You know him?" Jade shouldn't have been surprised, and had she been thinking clearly, she would have figured that if

Malcolm was thinking about Harrison & Talbot joining the Kahuna Group, Greg would know all about them. It was a partnership after all.

"Sure," Greg said. "I met him a few months after he, Cate, and Haley were back home. Jason came to the office and presented Gus's idea about the Kahuna Group. We chatted with Gus via video. Nice guy."

Jade nodded. She really liked Gus Tanaka.

"Neither Malcolm nor I have had time to discuss the details, but I think it's worth looking into."

She saw Greg slide a look at Malcolm, who nodded in return.

"Do you think an expert in art forgeries would be an asset to the group?" she blurted out.

"You're thinking this Smythe guy?" Malcolm asked.

"No, me actually. And Megan," she added with a nod in Greg's direction, trying to ignore Malcolm's narrowed eyes. "She's studying art, and all the time she's been with us, we've been teaching her as jobs came in." She lifted her shoulders in a shrug. "We'd make a great team, like you and Malcolm make a great team." *Just like Malcolm and I would,* Jade's heart whispered.

She glanced at Malcolm. His gaze was shuttered, his body ramrod stiff.

Damn, she shouldn't have blurted out anything. And yet, it was her life, her decision, and Jade reminded herself that she wasn't going to be controlled again, even if it was out of love and caring.

Love?

Shaking her head slightly over her mental choice of words, she realized that none of the self-talk eased the ache of disappointment settling around her heart. She studied her entwined fingers, knuckles white with tension.

Forcing herself to look at Greg, she saw the opposite reaction and her spirits rose again. And more interesting, he was puzzled at the reproving glance Malcolm gave her.

"Interesting idea. Have you run it past Meg?" Greg asked.

Jade shook her head. "No, I really only started thinking about it since Evan's death."

Greg got off his stool. "This has been hell for you, Jade, and I think this might be the answer." He patted the pocket that held the pendant. "I'll let you know the minute I can figure it out. I don't want to ruin the pendant. In fact I want to try and reverse the signal and find out who is getting the info. I'll be off. I haven't let Megan know I'm back." A thoughtful look came over his face, then worry. "I'll call her from the lab. If this is a transmitter of some sort, I don't want to go the cabin and lead them to her."

"Greg! You should have gone there first," Jade said with heat.

"I love my Meg, but she's safe and you're not. She'll understand. Let's get this solved."

Jade was folded in Greg's hug with a peck on the cheek. Then he waved to Malcolm and was out the front door before she could say goodbye.

Malcolm locked the door behind him.

"IS THIS THE IDEA THAT'S BEEN FLOWING THROUGH THE BACK OF your mind when I ask you what's up and you tell me 'later'?" Malcolm tried to keep his voice calm but heard the same tone he used on his brothers when he'd needed to be the parent.

Jade raised her chin in response. "Yes. I haven't thought it through yet, but it sounds like something I could do and do well."

Suddenly he was too close to her, swamped by memories of their kiss, and that only fired up his protective instincts. He needed distance and moved to the other side of the kitchen island. He didn't want to get mad, he wanted to be reasonable, even calm, and talk her out of it.

"I *am* an art expert," Jade stated in an even voice. "Evan was the best of the best and taught me well. I've been trained to observe, root out the fakes and copies. Instead of rebuilding Laurent Art Brokers, I could open a PI service for artwork. There is a huge demand, and while it would cost a pretty penny to buy the equipment needed, it wouldn't be impossible."

"You're serious about this?" He could tell by the sudden gleam of battle in her eyes he'd struck a nerve.

"Why not? And while I don't know anything about PI work—"

"Damn straight you don't, Little Miss Sleuth. It's a world filled with people who have need of a hired gun. And ninety-nine percent of the people I'm hired to find or tail have nasty and potentially dangerous secrets they don't want me to uncover. This isn't Nancy Drew, with Megan as Bess or George for a sidekick."

"But this is art. This isn't what Greg does. Or did before you called him back. How are you going to talk him out of active surveillance? The same way you're talking to me?"

Malcolm ignored that last part, though he acknowledged that he'd have a battle on his hands, just like now. Greg liked field work, but Malcolm hoped he loved his geeky side more. "And that art"—he let the word hang—"can be worth millions, didn't you say? With syndicates trying to pawn off forgeries? Do you think they're just going to let you expose them? This isn't a game. You could have your head shot off."

THE MEASURED TONES IN MALCOLM'S VOICE THAT BROOKED NO discussion shook Jade badly. She'd done nothing but throw out an idea, and he'd turned against her swiftly. Not bothering to hear her out, consider her position, but just condemning the whole idea and saying no.

Too much like her father and Evan. Though they always said no with velvet masking the steel.

"And what will you do if Greg doesn't want to be removed from active surveillance or undercover work? You're a partnership. You don't get to dictate." She took a deep breath and went on. "The same is true for me. Especially me. What I do with my life is now totally up to me. For the first time in my life, I"—she pointed to her chest—"*I* can make decisions based on what I want to do, not what someone else wants me to do or be. I loved my father and was willing to be what he wanted me to be. I enjoyed parts of the business, but being an art broker for the rest of my working days? No." Turning away, she scanned the room, looking for something that she could focus on instead of the disappointment that filled her. Her gaze found the window where they'd stood as they'd shared that soul-rocking kiss. A deep sigh escaped. There was no use pretending this hadn't changed everything back to PI and client. Perhaps that was best.

She faced him again. "I'd hoped we might have some sort of relationship once this was over. But not if you're going to over-protect me like you did with your brothers. You said you learned."

Unable to stand being in the same room with him, she jumped off the kitchen stool and fled to her borrowed bedroom.

What a great bloody fool I've been. Hadn't she just realized that the only way to be in control of her own life was to remain totally self-reliant and unattached emotionally to anyone, anything?

Obviously, she'd had a brain blockage ... or been lulled into forgetting.

The only thing she knew for certain was that she wasn't

going to reopen Laurent Art Brokers. That business had been her father's dream, not hers. He'd never known the real reason she'd willingly taken on the task of learning the business and the heavy mantle of future ownership. She would have done anything to please him since he'd sacrificed so much for her.

Love equaled sacrifice. Even Malcolm knew that. Independence equaled freedom of choice. Something he didn't get yet, even though it sounded as if his brothers had finally shown their own independence.

She drummed her fingers on the koa chest of drawers. She didn't need Malcolm. Maybe Greg would help her, and if not, she'd find somebody, maybe even Gus. Maybe she'd move to Hawaii. Why not? Megan would have been an ideal partner, but now, if she needed to move, she'd go solo. There was absolutely nothing now to keep her in Boulder, Colorado.

Not even Malcolm.

It never was Malcolm. He was just a moment. Conceived in the heat of danger and nurtured by proximity. Simple.

Tears blurred her vision, but she refused to let them fall. Dashing a quick hand over eyes and blinking several times, she could focus again.

If Greg had the pendant and it turned out that it held the clue as to why David was always one step ahead, then perhaps this could be over sooner rather than later. If not, she'd stick it out until it was. But she'd keep her distance emotionally.

Just the fact that she no longer wore the formerly beloved gift increased her sense of security. Maybe tomorrow she could go home. Though even her cherished home felt alien.

Maybe Hawaii would be a great new start. Then she remembered David's business was headquartered there. Paris?

Too many memories.

Never mind, she'd figure that out tomorrow.

16

MALCOLM PACED THE LIVING ROOM, WALKED DOWN THE HALL TO the bedroom Jade occupied, and back to the living room, his brain and heart in turmoil.

He'd totally bungled the entire conversation. His protective instincts had kicked into high gear. In fact, to be honest, they were in overdrive times ten.

What he'd stupidly forgotten, or maybe didn't want to face, was the knowledge that Jade could do whatever she wanted. And she'd made it clear that if he was so stubbornly pigheaded about this, she'd do it on her own.

Wouldn't it be better to make sure she had the right kind of people behind her, beside her? *Yeah, well, beside her may be a moot point now. You broke your cardinal rule. You got involved, and how. Your petite warrior just drew blood. And she wasn't likely to easily forgive.*

That was true. Hadn't she said "*What I do with my life is now totally up to me. For the first time in my life.*" She wasn't going to simply capitulate.

And while they just might have solved the *how* of this deadly stalking, there was more to uncover. He needed to see it through to the end.

If Jade hadn't decided to fire him.

Walking back to her bedroom, he knocked on the door. No answer.

"Jade, we need to talk, to clear the air."

Nothing. Then he heard soft footfalls and the door opened.

She stood, arms crossed, legs apart.

"Totally my picture of a petite warrior."

"So that wasn't a dream. You've called me that before?"

Malcolm lifted his shoulders in a shrug. "It fits."

Leaning against the door jam, he saw the emotions flicker across her face. From wariness to attention.

"I won't try and talk you out of this. But I will paint an unvarnished picture." He grinned at his own pun and got a small one from her in return. "A picture of the difficulties and the rewards of this kind of work."

She nodded and he was encouraged to continue. At least he wasn't shut out.

"I'm not trying to be anything other than true to me. It's the first idea I've been excited about in a long time." Jade uncrossed her arms and moved a step closer to him. "I can't go back to what I was. If, after this, there is anything left of the once impeccable reputation of Laurent Art Brokers, I can use it to build a clientele with some of the same people. They'll need what I can do for them if they continue to buy art."

Malcolm moved one step toward her. "It would be best if you could apprentice with someone, not for your expertise, but how to handle yourself in various situations."

"And that might be ... you?"

The hope in her voice lightened his heart. "Might be." He moved another step, putting them almost toe to toe. "Tomorrow might bring this to closure, but it won't be finally over until

David's gang is rounded up. I'm betting, however, that they are so far underground they'll slink right back down and we'll never find them. Unless he talks."

Malcolm didn't mention that something still niggled at the back of his consciousness, and he couldn't nail it down. But now wasn't the time to bring that up.

"I won't let anyone run my life."

He raised one brow. "Got it."

She mimicked his eyebrow raise.

"Promise," he said and received a queenlike nod in response, triggering another grin. "So, while we wait for Greg's report, which could take all night, or not, how about an Irish coffee, decaf, so we can both sleep tonight."

"Deal, but first—" She reached up and wrapped her arms around him, pulling his face close.

He captured her lips in another kiss, different from the earlier one as this one held a different promise. He hoped he was right and tomorrow was a new day with a whole new chapter to begin. Healing and moving forward.

Together.

He again felt the niggle, but for now, he let it be.

17

MONDAY BARELY DAWNED. THE SPRING HAD TURNED "COLORADO fickle" and clouds were building, threatening snow.

Jade, wearing sweats and slippers, held a cup of coffee in both hands, waiting for Malcolm to come back from his run. It was past ten and she should look in the fridge to see what she could whip up for breakfast.

He'd said he needed to figure out something and would be gone about an hour, that a run usually cleared his head and brought clarity. Jade hoped his clarity wasn't going to have him renege on his promise of helping her in a new career.

Maybe a hearty meal after the run would keep him mellowed out about it.

She heard her phone ding once, then again. Reluctantly leaving the unruly weather panorama before her, she put down her cup and headed to the bedroom where she'd left the phone on the bedside table.

The ding meant someone was at the door. Odd.

She brought up her camera, and Smythe stood there. He was supposed to be in Hawaii.

"Jade? Jade? I couldn't leave without seeing with my own

eyes you were safe. I saw the bombing on the news. I saw ambulances and firetrucks. I called the clients and told them I'd be on the one o'clock plane. They were fine with that. Jade? Are you there?"

She didn't need Smythe to screw up this order. It was now her last commission deal for him and they'd been paid handsomely for it. "Why aren't you in Hawaii? Go, you can see me now." Frustration totally blotted out the morning's quietness. She'd be glad to be done with this man.

"I just wanted to make sure you're okay. Don't be mad, please. You're my best link for commissions. I won't have a career without you."

He was talking so fast, he was barely intelligible. Worse, she saw the tears slide under his awful glasses and down his cheeks.

"Jade. Please. Just wave at me let me know you're okay and I'll go happily."

She marched to the window near the garage and front door. Smythe stood there, a few feet back from the window, hunched over, looking as pitiful as he sounded. She saw his Mercedes van parked near the garage.

"See me wave? Now go, before you miss your plane. We'll talk more, but later. Just don't worry. It will all work out. Promise."

Suddenly the window shattered, knocking her backward as bits of the double-paned glass showered down on her.

"Jade!"

Smythe stepped through the window and reached out a helping hand. She grasped it, realizing far too late that Smythe shouldn't have known her whereabouts at the safehouse.

Pulling her hand away from him, she scrabbled backward until he drew back his arm, then pistoned it forward. Stars exploded.

Then nothing.

～

RUNNING A TRAIL IN THE MOUNTAINS OR AROUND A PARK NEAR HIS condo in LoDo always cleared Malcolm's mind. It had to be outside, never on a treadmill. It was the fresh air with zero distractions that did the trick, helping him find those obscure missing links.

Most times. This time even with the fresh, now colder air with the massive mountain as a backdrop, he still couldn't pinpoint his feeling.

Glancing at his watch, he realized he needed to turn around. He'd promised Jade he'd be back around ten. He was fairly sure she was going to want to leave their borrowed digs today. He'd already had a team in to clean her house after the breach, including the fingerprinting powder. He hadn't told her because ...

Home.

Suddenly Malcolm had the missing piece.

He kicked in his last reserves and clocked world-class time flying down the trail. He reached the house and immediately saw the broken window and the charred debris and ground.

Frantically keying in the code, he stepped into the foyer and saw blood. His own ran cold. Then it turned icy when he saw the note, written in capital letters tacked up on the closet door.

BRING ANYONE WITH YOU AND JADE IS DEAD. COME ALONE AND YOU'LL HAVE ONE CHANCE TO SAVE HER. DON'T DALLY. WHEN YOU SEE THE MERCEDES VAN YOU'RE THERE.

Along with the note was a crude map. Up Sunshine Canyon. A twisty road, not easy to follow even in the best of conditions.

He checked the sky.

The flakes that had threatened earlier were beginning to fall, and the temperature was dropping, as was the light. Midmorning and already a spring blizzard was forming.

Grabbing a jacket and boots from his room, he forced himself to slow down and think. Weapon loaded? A quick double-check reassured him that his 9mm Glock was loaded, with one in the chamber, along with the knowledge that he had another clip in a hidden cache under the seat of his Range Rover. Now that he no longer needed the borrowed BMW to throw David's crew off his trail, he wanted his familiar vehicle. He knew the Rover's every quirk and hitch. How it responded to his touch. Every micro-second advantage could help him save Jade.

He shot down the driveway and onto the road, maneuvering with fierce concentration, cursing each red light, until he got onto the Sunshine Canyon Road and started following the instructions on the map.

JADE OPENED ONE EYE, THEN THE OTHER. HER HEAD ACHED BEYOND belief and she tried to raise her hands but couldn't. She realized they were bound with the same type of plastic cuffs that Malcolm had used on David.

"Glad to you see you're awake. I didn't want you to miss the entire show."

"What the hell are you doing, Smythe?"

"Making the circle complete."

"It was you the entire time?" *Smythe.* She'd never considered him.

"Yep. Wait just a minute, then I'll tell you more." He gripped the wheel and gently pumped the brakes.

The van swayed around the hairpin turn. The steep drop-off on her side caused her stomach to flip.

Jade fought the nausea from her headache and the motion of the van.

She glanced at him, still reeling from shock. Smythe. The hunched-over man with a high, squealing voice, glasses magnifying his frog eyes, concealed a killer.

"How'd you get me into the van?"

"Carried you."

That didn't make sense. How could he? With his deformed spine, he could barely handle the large paintings he'd brought to the office.

"Okay, ready?" he asked.

"No." Something wasn't right, but fear and the swaying of the van kept her from thinking clearly.

"Oh, I think you are. Don't you want to know the reason behind all this? I'm not telling unless you watch my show."

Watch his show? Smythe was clearly a gifted artist—was this all because he wanted fame in his own name and not simply that of a reproduction genius? Then why didn't he just do it? Why steal the Khan, murder Evan and perhaps her father and Omarr? Nothing made sense.

The van slid again on the treacherous road and vomit rose in her throat, burning all the way up. Cupping her mouth with her bound hands, she forced herself to swallow the bile.

She turned toward him, anything to distract him while she tried thinking of ways to escape. "We can have a one-man show. I had no idea you wanted that."

His high-pitched laughter chilled her core, and he glanced her way, his eyes bulging behind the thick lenses.

"Watch out," she screamed, pointing to a car sticking out from the shoulder of the road, fully covered in snow, barely visible in the wind-whipped whiteness.

Smythe swerved, just missing the car, and jerked the wheel hard to get the van back to the road.

Her head banged on the side window, and she closed her eyes against the pain.

Finally the van stopped, and Jade opened her eyes.

"We're here. Now for the show."

Confusion and ice-cold fear penetrated every cell in her body.

Smythe removed his glasses. He glanced at her. Something wasn't right. No frog eyes.

"Got it yet? No? Okay, next."

Then he yanked off his wig and spit out some sort of mouth guard.

She didn't need for him to turn around. "Aksel?" Her voice broke on the name.

"Yes, you got it, *ma chérie*."

18

WIND BEGAN TO BLOW THE SNOWFLAKES HORIZONTALLY, AND visibility grew steadily worse. *One chance, one chance, one chance to save her,* played in Malcolm's mind in rhythm with the Rover's windshield wipers, torturing him as he navigated the twisty mountain road up Sunshine Canyon. What would he find once he reached Jade?

Turning on his headlights, he swore loudly. They only illuminated the area ahead into a whiteout. He fishtailed around a double-hairpin turn and fought the wheel as the SUV momentarily lost traction. The pavement ended. The road turned into a muddy quagmire under the onslaught of the spring snowstorm. Wet snowflakes clung to every surface, obliterating any depth of field. He slowed to a crawl, scanning each van parked in a driveway for that Mercedes star symbol. Twice he had to get out and brush off the wet snow on the back of the vans to check.

Malcolm worked out the detail lurking at the back of his mind too late. The cigarette in the picture on her mantel, the one Aksel held, was the same type of cigarette they found in Evan's kitchen sink. That was the strong and distinctive smell.

Too late, too late, too late, the windshield wipers played in cadence with his fear. "No, he's waiting for me," Malcolm yelled. He needed to pull it together, be totally in control so he could handle whatever came up.

His adrenaline surge wasn't allowing that to happen.

THE WORLD OUTSIDE THE VAN CEASED TO EXIST IN THE BLOWING whiteness. Jade's world consisted of Aksel, herself, and her overwhelming fear.

Cold settled deep into her heart as she thought of never again seeing Malcolm's cerulean eyes crinkle with a smile, never experiencing the joy of his deep laugh, his intoxicating kisses. Never exploring the future together.

Those thoughts were the only thing she could grasp.

No. Pushing those thoughts back, Jade knew she needed Aksel to talk to buy them time. Malcolm was coming. She knew that somehow he'd figure out where to look for her. "Where are we?"

"It's a beautiful cabin, yes?" He pointed through the blowing snow to a large, modern log cabin.

She started to shake her head but stopped when shards of pain poked into her skull again.

"Seriously, you're ruining my fun. This is where Smythe created his magnificent reproductions. I'm kind of sorry to let that persona go." He shrugged. "Maybe I won't after all."

"But—"

"Ssshhh. I know what you're doing. Time to stop talking." He put a finger to her lips, and she moved quickly, trying to bite hard. But he was faster or had anticipated her reaction.

He wagged the same finger at her. "I've been waiting two years for this. I've had a long time to put everything into motion.

Do you know how easy it is to hire dangerous people on the dark web? I think you do, now. Your Malcolm will not be able to rescue you. Oh, he'll try, but he'll watch you die and be helpless to act. Then he'll follow you to hell."

"Follow? You plan on killing Malcolm?" she whispered. Horror tightened her throat.

"But of course. I left him a map. Didn't you figure it out? He has to go too, and it's all because of you. You brought him in. When I saw all the security and that you weren't alone, I couldn't take the chance that you'd told him enough that he could put it all together. So you'll be responsible for his death."

Her heartbeat hammered and she couldn't suck in enough air. Blackness clouded her vision.

A sharp, stinging slap snapped her head sideways, clearing her panic and replacing it with consuming fury.

Malcolm was coming and he'd be prepared. If he'd gotten a note, he'd know the killer would be waiting for him, and he wouldn't fall into Aksel's trap. She had to believe that.

He would be smarter than Aksel. He had better skills than Aksel.

She would not die at the hands of Aksel.

Neither would Malcolm.

"We were friends," she said to the man beside her.

"And you're naïve." He got out of the van and came around to her side. Sliding open the side panel, he pulled out something, then slammed the side door shut. With a satisfied smile, he opened her door. "One foot at a time. Slowly, *chérie*."

She did as he said. He removed one of her slippers, slid on a clunky snow boot, laced it up, then gestured for her other foot. Oddly, the boots fit. Then she realized—of course they would. As he said, he'd planned it well with time to consider every detail.

"Too bad I can't trust you not to do something rash if I

remove your bonds." He nodded toward her wrists. "No coat for you. You'll just have to be cold. It won't bother you for long. Get out."

Jade stepped out into the blizzard.

"Move." Aksel prodded her with something hard.

She looked over her shoulder. A gun filled her vision. *Malcolm would be smarter than Aksel. He had better skills than Aksel,* played in her heart, a mantra born of need.

There was nothing she could do but comply, advancing one unsteady foot forward, then the other. The cold wind sliced through her sweats like scissors through tissue.

They passed the big cabin where Smythe/Aksel worked and headed down a steeply wooded hill. The trees offered a slight break from the wind, but their roots and branches became their own obstacles for her, snagging either a boot or her shirt. There was no way she could catch herself with the wrist bonds. And when she fell, Aksel made no effort to help her up, so she struggled, her already chilled hands pressing into the deepening snow to push herself upright. "Ow!"

"*Chérie?*"

She saw the blood on her right palm, oozing from a deep and ragged gash. Looking down, Jade saw the red smear in the snow. She'd cut herself on a sharp rock buried in the snow.

She held her bound, bleeding palms toward Aksel, but he merely looked at them and grinned. "The blood'll make him worry. I should have thought it of myself."

"It doesn't matter, he'll never find us. Our footsteps are already being covered by the snow. While you have me, you'll never get him."

Aksel turned to look up the steep slope and then back at her. She saw his madman's brain at work, his lips pursing and flattening as he thought and discarded ideas. Then finally came that sick smile.

"We'll just have to make sure he knows where to go. Move, but in a shuffle, making a trail for him. I'll do the same. He'll see it even though it's still snowing."

They continued their solitary journey through the forest of ponderosa pines and bare aspens. Visibility dropped as the wind gusted, sending a blanket of snow into her face. Jade slowed as her body temperature fell. Despair nearly overwhelmed her.

Just as suddenly, the wind died. For a moment, the quiet and beauty of the snow-blanketed forest was a surreal counterpoint to the danger she was in.

That Malcolm was walking into.

No, she wouldn't give up. Ever. Then, as if to mock her resolve, a blast of wind and snow swirled around her, destroying her brief respite.

"Stop." Aksel spoke sharply. "Turn around and back up two steps."

Jade looked wildly at Aksel, uncertain what he was asking of her.

"Do it, *ma chérie*."

"Never call me that again." She'd never hated anyone as she did him in the moment.

"That's an easy request." He shrugged in that once-charming Gallic way.

She followed his eerie directions. Then her childhood friend calmly sat down on a tree stump several feet away and pointed that very lethal gun at her. Jade took another step back, intent on leaving this nightmare, sure he couldn't really pull the trigger.

"One more step and you will save me the trouble of shooting you."

She stopped mid step and looked over her shoulder to find the yawning mouth of an abandoned mine shaft. Vertigo from the cold and fear that even her mantra couldn't assuage swamped her. She swayed with dizziness, falling backward toward the abyss.

Strong arms steadied her.

"Why did you save me when you want me dead?" Jade cried, confused and terrified.

"Ah, *ma chérie*." He raised a questioning brow. "Don't you want to know why I killed my dad, your father, Evan, and now you? And of course your dear Malcolm?"

19

TEN MILES FURTHER UP THE CANYON, MALCOLM FOUND THE VAN. Slowly driving past, staring hard through the heavily falling snow, he noted there were no tracks that led to the modern log cabin. Two faint sets appeared to lead away from the cabin, then disappeared as the terrain seemed to slope downward. He backed in, deliberated blocking the van, then decided to park beside it, knowing they might need a quick getaway.

Only the disciplined act of rechecking his clip and securely settling his 9mm into his waistband's paddle holster allowed him to fight back his urge to run blindly to Jade's rescue.

Any emotion would nullify his ability to act with precision. And when he reached them, any hint of affection for Jade would reveal a vulnerability Aksel would certainly capitalize on.

Without a plan and no chance of backup, Malcolm tied his boots and shrugged on his jacket, then stepped out into the spring blizzard. The frozen crystals stung his cheeks and eyes, blinding him for a moment. Hands up to protect his face, he crossed the short distance to the van. Placing his hand on the hood, he still felt warmth, so hopefully they hadn't traveled far.

Brushing off the quickly accumulating snow, he checked the

van through the front windows but saw nothing that gave him any clue to Aksel's plan.

He began to follow two faint sets of tracks that led down into a steep valley.

The blizzard allowed for only dull light to penetrate the deepness of the forest. For the first hundred yards, he struggled to find the tracks. The snow and wind obliterated all but the deepest indentations, making them invisible a few feet away. Backtracking was taking too long. The light faded as the storm gathered intensity. The cold was vicious and the wind exacerbated it. Malcolm prayed that Jade had on winter gear, that Aksel wasn't that cruel, but knew that was false hope. The man was insane.

A sharp crack sounded.

Malcolm swiveled and crouched, reaching for his gun. He quickly scanned the area, only to see a shower of snow falling from a bough that snapped under the weight of the heavy snowfall. Not breathing, listening intently just to be sure, he waited until he could no longer hold it in, and sucked in a lungful of frigid air.

Then he continued on, driven by fear for Jade's life.

AH, MA CHÉRIE, DON'T YOU WANT TO KNOW WHY I KILLED DAD, YOUR father, Evan, and now you? And his cruel addition of Malcolm. Aksel's arrogant confession vibrated through Jade. Though he'd just saved her from toppling backward into the mine, he was simply toying with her. He'd sealed her fate with his admission. Did she want to hear his crazed reasons? What justification could he possibly have for destroying the lives of three people? And now two more?

"There is nothing you can say that will justify your actions. You murdered—"

"Be quiet and hear my side of the story." He caressed the side of her cheek with the barrel of his gun. Then he stepped back to his stump, the gun aimed directly at her heart, his finger poised to pull the trigger. "You know I didn't want to move to America."

Jade was shivering so hard she could barely nod.

"I love Paris, and the gallery always had its 'special clients.' You know those who wanted a Manet, no matter how they got it?"

She couldn't answer. The horror of what he was suggesting closed her throat. Jade swung her head sideways in disbelief. "No, they stopped years ago—"

"Your father told you about their, shall I say, hobby?"

"No."

"Of course not, your father would never tell his precious little Jade anything that might be uncomfortable."

That was true, part of the protective swaddling she'd recently shed. But she was certain they had no idea that their past could lead to all this death.

"But because they stopped didn't mean I didn't learn from them. You said it yourself—I am a master reproduction artist. My dear father became a bit suspicious that I was doing more than merely reproducing art. He questioned one of my most trusted vendeuses. She of course didn't mean to, as you say, spill the beans. But she did. Naturally, she paid for it with a swim in the Seine."

So Aksel had killed before taking Omarr's life. Her hope dwindled. This was four murders ...

"My father told me he was closing the galleries. I didn't believe him at first, but when I realized he was determined to do so, I had to stop him. I was getting very rich. You know how much fools will pay for an undiscovered piece by a master? Millions. And they'll never tell a soul about it, for fear it will be repossessed by some country or estate it was plundered from. You know the type.

"So, Father, or Père as I preferred to call him, had a heart attack. Pretty simple to do."

He looked so self-satisfied, as if he were talking about a minor deed, not cold-blooded and heartless murder.

"The galleries were mine. Until your father received the letter my father sent him just before he perished, explaining my ... expanded role in the business. The idea of the anniversary dates came into my mind. And I loved it. A year ago, it was your father's time, but it couldn't be a heart attack. I ran him over. Simple."

"Why didn't Dad expose you?"

"He thought about it, but I simply told him if he did, I'd kill you."

Her heart ached more for her father. His sudden security issues were now explained. *Why didn't he get a professional involved? Because it would have revealed their past.*

She wondered if her beloved papa had any idea that Aksel was behind the wheel when the car hit.

"He knew, *chérie*."

"You're a bastard, you slimy, disgusting—"

"Rich."

"Murdering coward."

Aksel shook his head. "Your Malcolm is late."

Jade knew that but needed to keep him talking, so maybe Malcolm would hear them before he was seen. "But why Evan?"

"He knew because he'd seen my work in the apartment over the gallery. I swore to him that it was just for fun. I really didn't think he'd believe me, and I knew sooner or later he'd find more proof. It's what he did.

"His was the most interesting death. Curare. Rare, but not

unattainable. Once I knew that Evan had told you about his connection with the FBI and our fathers' works—"

"Nobody told me, Aksel. I found out from Malcolm's firm."

Aksel's gun wavered for a moment.

"All this for money and fame." She'd pushed too hard. The gun he held steadied as his eyes narrowed and his lips tightened into a ruthless sneer.

"You weren't listening. Money. Not fame. In a year or maybe two, I'll close the remaining Paris gallery and just live the perfect Parisian life."

FEELING HE WAS GETTING CLOSER AS THE TERRAIN WAS LEVELING out a bit, Malcolm slowed, carefully avoiding any noise, until he saw blood-smeared snow. His hands shook with uncontrolled fury. Blackness filled his heart. He was too late, and Aksel was going to hide her body in whatever hellish place he'd picked for her to die.

A howl of rage burst from Malcolm. Belatedly he regained his self-control. He'd blown what little advantage he'd had.

A HUMAN HOWL RENT THE AIR. IT HAD TO BE MALCOLM, FINDING the bloodied snow. Aksel had been right. The sight had broken Malcolm, and worse, had revealed that he was close by.

She opened her mouth to scream.

"Don't, or I'll shoot you right now. I offered a chance to your PI to save you, but you'll ruin it all."

She shut up. This man was crazy. She had to believe that once Malcolm found them, they could escape. He was smarter than Aksel. He wasn't crazy like the man in front of her.

Aksel leisurely rose from his seat on the tree stump and moved to stand next to her. "Come out, Mr. Talbot, and say hello," he yelled into the quiet.

Then he wrapped an arm around her throat and pressed the gun against her temple.

Whatever reserves of strength she had were used up. The cold made her sluggish and the adrenaline of fear couldn't push through it.

It was up to Malcolm to keep them alive.

MALCOLM FOLLOWED AKSEL'S SUDDENLY PRONOUNCED FRENCH accent until he gauged that he was close enough to take the shot. There was no use regretting his tipping the madman off. It was done. Now he had to work to save Jade despite that additional handicap.

For in that moment of fear, he realized that he didn't simply feel affection for her, it was heart-pounding love. And damn if he was not going to have the time to convince her that love could be freeing. It didn't have to wrap her in swaddling as she'd experienced.

He pulled out his gun, bringing it up, finger near the trigger, ready if the moment presented itself. Then he edged up behind a fir tree and risked a glance.

Aksel held Jade hostage with his gun to her head, an arm around her neck, holding her tightly against him.

She wore only the sweats she'd had on this morning and boots. No jacket, hat, or gloves. Even in Aksel's deadly embrace, he could see her shivering. For the moment that was a good sign. It was when one stopped shivering that the body signaled it was giving up.

Then the next realization hit. Jade and Aksel were standing

in front of an old mine. He saw part of the old decking that would have supported machinery or men to be lowered into the depths. What he didn't know was if the mine was boarded up or grated, but he guessed it was neither now. A perfect place to hide bodies.

Pulling in every ounce of the self-control that had abandoned him earlier, he surveyed the nightmare scene before him. He knew he only had one shot, and it was a risky shot at best. If he were behind Aksel, he could try for that sweet spot just under the curve of the skull that would drop him without the chance of his pulling the trigger in a death reflex.

But that wasn't the case here. Malcolm could shoot Aksel in the center of his forehead, and the bastard could still have that split second to pull the trigger. And when he fell, it could be backward into the mine, pulling Jade with him. An unacceptable risk.

Malcolm had to first try and lull Aksel into relaxing, moving the gun away from Jade's temple. Or at the very least, distract him by making him talk. "Let her go, Aksel. You can't kill both of us—"

JADE RECOILED IN AKSEL'S GRASP ONLY TO HAVE THE AIR CHOKED from her throat as his grip tightened. "Why would you think that? I can and I will. You first, then Jade. She'll have the short-lived pleasure of watching you die."

Time accelerated. Malcolm stepped from around the tree. The hard, cold steel ruthlessly pressed against her temple lifted as Aksel pointed his gun at him.

Jade gathered all her flagging strength and pushed against her captor. At the same time, with a strength born of desperation, she tried to fling herself forward. But his tight grip on her neck didn't loosen.

A sharp report pierced the air beside her ear, deafening her, and she prayed that Aksel's shot went wild. Wood cracked and splintered beneath their feet, giving way.

His grip around her neck slackened as he flailed his arms, trying to regain his balance on the rotten wooden boards covering the mine shaft.

She twisted hard but slid down the shaft following Aksel.

20

Terrified screams echoed off the steep hillsides.

Then deadly silence pressed in on Malcolm, stalling his breath, paralyzing any movement. Jade had disappeared right before his eyes, saving his life at the immeasurable cost of her own.

His lungs filled and he bounded through the snow drifts. At the mouth of the mine shaft, he knelt and looked into the black void. A jolt of sickening reality hit him—there was no way a person could have survived that fall.

Yet, his mind played tricks on him as he saw a pale mirage hover against the wall of the shaft. Malcolm scrambled around the splintered wooden opening to get a better look.

It was no mirage. Jade was dangling beneath a timber beam.

"Jade? Damnit, answer me!"

"Malcolm," Jade answered, her voice weak and thready.

She had survived. Against all odds, she had survived. But she had to be fading quickly.

"Can you tell me what you're ... caught on?"

"I can't tell, something snagged the cable on my wrists."

Malcolm couldn't even imagine the pain she was enduring on top of the bitter cold.

"I'm afraid to move."

He stretched out on the frozen ground and inched as far forward into the mouth of the shaft as possible. He reached down, and searing pain radiated up his right arm. Malcolm didn't have to look to know Aksel's bullet had done more than graze his shoulder.

Reaching down with his left arm, Malcolm's fingers touched Jade's. "There, can you feel me?"

"Malcolm, I can't feel anything. My fingers are numb."

Despite the bone-chilling cold, fear covered him in a fine sweat. If she couldn't grasp his hand, he had to get a good enough hold on her so she wouldn't slip away when he pulled her to the surface. That meant grabbing the nylon strap. Not only would the pain be horrendous, but the small gap between her bound wrists that he had to hold on to allowed no mistakes.

Malcolm Talbot couldn't lose her now. Somehow he would find the strength to pull her up with one arm.

"Jade?" Sweet Jesus! Why didn't she say something?

"Malcolm."

Thank you, his soul whispered. "Honey, I'm going to reach down. I don't want you to move right now, okay? I'm going to grasp the middle of the cable between your wrists. I won't lie, it's going to hurt like hell. I'm going to pull you up, so try to stay away from whatever is snagging you as you come up. But don't wiggle too much, okay?"

"Okay, not move. My shoulders feel like they're going to pop out."

God, the pain she must be in. Time was running out. She could lose consciousness from the combination of hypothermia and trauma.

There was no more time and no room for doubts. "This is going to work. Ready?"

"Y-yes."

"On the count of three. One … two … three." Malcolm stretched as far as he could. He felt Jade's fingers again, then grabbed hold of the nylon cord between her wrists, giving him a more secure handle. Her sharp gasp of pain as the cord cut into her ripped through him. Pulling her up a bit, she was suddenly freed from the hook, and his arm nearly tore out of its socket as her full weight sagged against his grasp.

For a split second, Malcolm was able to hold her, then her weight dragged them both downward.

"Malcolm," she screamed.

He dug into the snow with his feet, trying to anchor himself. Adrenaline pumped through him, and he slowly inched Jade upward until he couldn't lift any further with one arm. Teeth gritted against the debilitating pain in his wounded shoulder, he grabbed and wrested her free of the deadly hole.

His Jade was alive.

Without warning, a red haze clouded his vision, and he blacked out.

SHE LAY ABOVE GROUND, FACE DOWN IN THE SNOW, MALCOLM sprawled across her. He'd saved her. They were alive.

For a few moments Jade lay still, expecting him to move off her. "Malcolm?"

He didn't answer.

Jade summoned an ounce of strength and craned her neck to check on him. She stared with horror as blood flowed from his shoulder, a scarlet stain spreading rapidly in the dirty, trampled snow. Aksel's bullet had found its mark.

She tried to roll from underneath Malcolm, but her flagging strength was no match for his dead weight. "Malcolm, damnit, answer me," she yelled as loud as she could manage, echoing the words he'd used only moments ago. He couldn't die now. They were safe.

His weight shifted. "We made it, sweetheart," he murmured as he struggled to sit upright.

She pushed upward using her elbows, then rose to her knees and leaned backward until she sat. Now they could at least face each other. "How bad is it?"

He shook his head. "Jade, the Rover is at the top of the road."

She knew getting up the hill was going to be the final test of endurance for both of them.

"If I pass out again, get the keys out of my pocket and keep going. Don't wait for me to regain consciousness, just keep going. You have to get to some warmth. Frostbite."

She held his gaze, refusing to accept his edict, knowing by the time she got back with help, he could be dead.

He pulled the phone from his pocket. "No signal, but I activated the 911 beacon. They'll find me if you have to move on."

"No, we're going to make this. Yes, we're both in terrible shape. But I'm not giving up now."

"I'd give you my jacket, but I can't get it off without—"

"Then let's start moving."

Malcolm clumsily got to his feet and then helped her up with his good arm. She knew it took far more energy than he had just to accomplish this small action.

With his good arm around her, leaning on each other, they started climbing the steep hill. One foot in front of the other, the biting wind pushing against them, an enemy that could prove as fatal as Aksel.

Jade fought the numbing need to rest, knowing she was close to hypothermia. Sleep meant death. And Malcolm couldn't drag her up the hill. Time had no reality. Their world revolved around simply putting step after step and moving upward through the forest.

They reached the last steep climb, and the trees thinned. They'd been in such a microcosm of fear and pain, it was odd to see a normal world outside that envelope of just surviving. To realize that a blizzard still raged. "Another dozen yards, Malcolm. So close, we'll make it."

Then she slipped, bringing Malcolm down with her. For a moment she feared he fainted again. He struggled to his feet, helping her up, and step by step they made the last bit of the trek.

Malcolm got them into the Rover and turned on the heater full blast. Pulling out his phone he called 911, told them the address, that he'd set a beacon earlier and that there were two victims alive and one dead.

Then he leaned back in the seat, his head against the headrest. "I can't drive, Jade. I'd kill us for sure. If I black out ..."

She couldn't feel anything in her hands. Holding a steering wheel was impossible, let alone the fact they were still bound by that bloodied nylon cable. It had saved her life, but she wanted it off with a fierceness that drove her to make one more effort before she collapsed. "You packed a gun, how about a knife?"

He rolled his head to face her. "In the glove box. Gimme a minute and I'll see if I can get it, but don't know how I'll—"

His words slurred and stopped. He toppled toward her, and she was able to just break his fall with her shoulder. He was losing so much blood. "Hang on, Malcolm, please. They'll come soon."

They have to.

21

THE PARAMEDICS MADE AMAZING TIME UP THE CANYON.

With the help of one of them, Jade shuffled the few feet to the ambulance, but Malcolm was still unconscious. She watched as the two medics lifted him onto a gurney and strapped him down. Soon, she and Malcolm were both settled in the back of the emergency vehicle and heading toward the hospital.

Jade saw the IV but was too numb to feel the puncture of the needle. She only realized blankets were tucked around her when the ambulance hit a bad bump, and she wakened enough to see the dark blue covers. The paramedic in the back with them watched her vitals, then would turn around and work on Malcolm.

With an effort, she roused herself and stayed awake, worrying about Malcolm. Jade couldn't see what the medic was doing for him and couldn't hear anything other than the siren. Yet she took a small measure of comfort that he didn't seem frantic as he worked over the man she loved. That had to be good news. She held onto that thought the entire ride down the canyon.

At Boulder Community Health, Boulder's hospital, Malcolm was wheeled in first. Jade desperately tried to get a glimpse of him, but except for a one-nanosecond glance, when the chalkiness of his face scared her to her core, the trauma team surrounding him made it impossible.

Jade reached for him, needing his touch, wanting to give him her strength as he'd always done for her.

But he was wheeled away with the team still working on him.

Moments later her gurney was maneuvered into an emergency cubicle.

Later, snugly cocooned in a Bair Hugger warm-air blanket, her shivers eased and eventually stopped, but her hands and legs now stung with needles of pain. She was given an antibiotic shot as a guard against infection from both the deep gash and the frostbite, and a painkiller IV drip along with a prescription to fill later. The ER doctor warned her that in a few days she should expect blisters to develop from her frostbite, but luckily the damage hadn't gone deep. Her shoulders ached, but surprisingly she hadn't dislocated anything.

She dozed in the warmth of the Bair Hugger, the drugs giving her a sense of both speeding and calm. An odd swirl of up and down.

"Ms. Laurent?"

She drifted upward on the spiral and opened her eyes to focus on a blue-scrub-clad person. She focused on her name tag. All she saw was the Dr. The rest didn't make any sense. It was just letters.

"Mr. Talbot asked that I give you an update on his condition."

Jade fought the drugs to be cognizant. She nodded to the doctor and held up her hand, seeing the thick layers of bandages. "He's okay?"

"He's out of surgery and in recovery. He'll stay here a couple of days so we can watch for complications. The bullet caused extensive damage to his shoulder, and he lost a lot of blood. He knows he'll need therapy. He asked to see you. If we get a wheelchair for you, can you see him?"

"Try and keep me away," Jade said on a feeble grin and got a thumbs up from the doc.

She waited impatiently as they brought the chair, transferred her IV to the tall hook on its back of, and tucked blankets around her. Into an elevator and down a hall. The rubber wheels of the chair squeaked as she was wheeled past Officer Arnold and Detectives Tomba and Moore in the waiting room on Malcolm's floor. They watched her silently.

Had they tried to stop her, she would have raised hell. However, seeing them cleared the last of her drug-induced calm and she couldn't get Aksel's screams out of her head. Tears burned and she fought them back. So many lives destroyed by his twisted mind.

To fight the horror, she concentrated on seeing Malcolm.

The orderly wheeled her into the glass cubicle. She hadn't realized Malcolm was in some sort of intensive care. How badly hurt was he? The doc had said he wanted to see her. How was that possible? Malcolm lay still under the white sheets, his bloodless features blending with the pillow. The only color was his dark hair and eyelashes. Panic rose in her chest. "Are you sure he's okay?"

"Yes, ma'am, this is standard procedure for the next twenty-four hours to monitor his vitals."

The orderly left her and, as prepared as she was about his condition, Malcolm's lifeless appearance shocked her. The low hum of the machines monitoring his vitals assured her he was being watched. The only monitor she knew to focus on in the vast array was the heartbeat blip. It looked steady.

"Jade."

She turned from the bank of monitors to see Malcolm's eyes open. Drugs dulled their intense blue slightly. And his voice–oh, his sweet voice–was nothing more than a hoarse whisper. Regardless, hearing him speak was the best gift she could have received.

"Can you come closer?"

Getting out the wheelchair and removing the cocoon of blankets with her bandaged hands and an IV took some time. But finally she stood at the edge of his bed.

"Closer."

She bent over the bed rails so her face was inches from him. His breath caressed her cheeks. He raised his head slightly and covered her mouth with a kiss that shattered her soul. Then he fell back against the pillows, his eyes closed.

Jade panicked for a moment and swiftly checked the monitor, relieved by its steady green blips.

He drifted in and out of awareness. The nurses came and checked on him frequently, and Jade was in their way. But each time he awakened, he immediately sought her presence, and they allowed her to stay, bringing in a chair that would be more comfortable and checking on her IV.

She had no idea of the time. She dozed when Malcolm did, and when the pain of her frostbite and the stitches in her palm became more than she could tolerate, they offered her more drugs. She asked for the lowest dosage possible, not wanting that up and down spiral again.

All she knew was that both she and Malcolm had survived. The case was over, finished in the grisliest way possible.

David wasn't at fault, though Evan's part in the stone's disappearance needed to be cleared up. But right now nothing mattered but Malcolm. She wasn't sure about any future with him. After all, she knew that love wasn't without its own ties. And she'd just shed one swaddling cloth.

"I love you, Jade Laurent."

She heard his molasses voice, stronger, clearer. Thank God.

Getting up from the lounge chair, she shuffled over to him.

"You heard me?"

She nodded.

"But?"

She swallowed hard. She loved this man, but he was a controller of people. He admitted it himself.

"If you'd die for me, why won't you live for me, Jade Laurent?"

Throwing herself against Aksel to save Malcolm hadn't been a conscious thought. She'd reacted the only way she could to protect the man she loved fiercely.

As she studied the face of the man she cherished, new understanding burgeoned. The lesson she'd learned from her father wasn't that love was filled with sacrifice and pain. His disillusionment had come from finding out the woman he worshiped had feet of clay. He'd become bitter with himself. Not at love.

You chose to stay with Laurent Art Brokers. You did everything your father asked because you would do anything for him, but Dad never asked it of you. You did it because you loved him and thought that was what he wanted.

Much of her swaddling cloth had been of her own making.

"I love you, Malcolm. With every fiber of my being."

"I hear the 'but' in your voice. I've heard enough of it in the past few days, to know it when I hear it."

She smiled slightly and saw his smile, if only for a second or two.

"There is only day by day and our love. I'm no expert on

relationships, Jade. I love you and I'm willing to make this work. Stay with me, be my partner in life."

He touched her face, then held up his left hand. Trusting him and her new-found wisdom, Jade grasped her future in both her thickly bandaged hands. Knowing her life would be empty without him. It was time to commit.

"Partners in life, my love."

22

As far as David Cole knew, he'd never met Aksel. The only reason any of them could come up with was that by framing him extra hurt would be added to Jade. That Aksel must have seen them together and assumed they were a couple.

David never got his phone back, but he did bring in a new phone with a copy of his dealings with Evan to Malcolm's office. As far as the Kublai Khan, there on the screen was Evan's signature that he indeed had given David the gem to return to its people. There was also a voice memo from her mentor.

David left them to listen to it alone. Jade leaned back in Malcolm's left arm—his right was still in a sling. She braced herself to hear the voice of a beloved friend, mentor, and second father.

"Jade, this was the hardest thing I've done. To go back on our word. The Kublai Khan must go back to its people. The curse is real, at least I and David believe it to be. He will be returning the stone to its rightful place and hopefully can make peace with his mother. I hope that this recording never plays and I get to tell you all this in person. But if not, beware of Aksel. There is evil in his soul. Stay away from him. Above all find a life that gives you joy. You were as much my daughter as Gerard's, though he'd have fought me over that statement. Yours forever, Evan."

Tears coursed down Jade's cheeks, and Malcolm gently wiped them away. Minutes later, she opened the door and handed David back his phone. He said nothing, just took it and left. There really was nothing more to be said between them.

"Evan was protecting you," Malcolm said softly.

"He was. And I can't, won't, blame him for doing this. I don't think Mrs. Cole will want to publicly bring up the fact that 'my courier' failed in his duty either, as her son who indeed paid for the stone is returning it to its people. So I think that is all we'll hear about the Khan."

Her hands still ached, and it was difficult at times to concentrate. But she and Malcolm had agreed he'd tutor her and Megan in the art and science of the PI world. Megan had convinced Greg this was a path she wanted as well. Together they'd form a new Laurent business.

Jade's pendant now rested in a safety deposit box. She never intended to wear it again, but it deserved to be enjoyed for the beautiful piece of jewelry it was. She had feelers out to various museums and would decide on which one to donate it to once she had their answers.

She and Malcolm were contacting Gus at the Kahuna Group's new offices later this afternoon. The future never looked so promising.

~ The End ~

Thank you for reading *Brushed By Betrayal*. I truly hope you enjoyed. If so, I'd deeply appreciate your review. Our success in this incredibly competitive world relies on, yep, reviews.
Again, thank you.

LETTER TO MY READERS

Readers often ask me how I find stories to write. My answer may sound simplistic, but it's true, I get inspiration from life, news, conversations. I owned a custom jewelry business with my mother who has her master's degree and taught metalsmithing, and my father who was a scientist and flew around the world buying gems when he could.

When we as a family traveled with dad, he'd do his scientist thing and mom would haul me and my brother to galleries, cathedrals and museums. One time in Prague during the Soviet occupation, I mistakenly pushed the USSR translation button instead of the USA button. You can imagine the looks, and that we hightailed it out of there.

So *Brushed By Betrayal* was born by these experiences. It was originally entitled *Betrayal of the Trust*, but the book has morphed dramatically from those first attempts.

I'm very careful with my research, but did take a few liberties with the Khan. However, the gift of a stone to the most worthy son is, as far as history knows, true.

I hope you enjoyed the second book in the Kahuna Group

Series. If so, please leave a review either on the site where you purchased the book, at Goodreads and BookBub. We authors

Also, on my website, www.lasartor.com, you can find the book in the "Book Shelf" page and find pictures of cacao, how it grows, and what it looks as a pod and bean.

And I have a newsletter that I enjoy writing and sending monthly. Keeping you up to date on my writing, my crazy busy life and often my photography. And don't forget I love hearing from you! www.lasartor.com/contact-me.

ALSO BY L.A. SARTOR

STAR LIGHT ~ STAR BRIGHT SERIES

A Romantic Christmas Series Set In Snowy Boulder, Colorado

Be Mine This Christmas Night

Forever Yours This New Year's Night

Believe In Me This Christmas Morn

Dream Of Me This Christmas Eve

THE CARSWELL ADVENTURE SERIES

Heart Pounding Adventure With A Dash of Romance Set In Exotic Locales

Stone Of Heaven

Viking Gold

THE KAHUNA GROUP SERIES

Suspense With A Dash of Romance

Dare To Believe

Brushed By Betrayal

THE PLANTATION SERIES

Pure Romance Set in Costa Rica On A Rare Cacao Plantation

Prince Of Granola

THE JENNA HART JEWELRY MYSTERIES

A Cozy Mystery Series Set in the Colorado Ski Town Of Angelcroft

Tick Tock Dead (coming soon)

*Capture the code with a mobile device's QR reader to see all of
L.A. Sartor's Books*

ACKNOWLEDGMENTS

No author works alone. If we're lucky, we have a team behind us working to make our books better.

Audra Harders, Author extraordinaire and best beta reader in the world. We started writing novels at nearly the same time, and it's been an amazing journey, my friend.

Ellis Vidler, My tireless editor who gets me and my stories, thank goodness. Thank you for everything you fight through to polish my books.

Amanda Cabot, Thank you for your help with the title and other aspects of the book.

The Book Babes, A trio of authors, who believes we can create magic with our stories. After all isn't that what great books do? XO Nancy Haddock and Neringa Bryant.

CORE Group, Five authors who meet every two weeks to encourage and improve any part of my writing process that I bring to the meeting, and will just listen if that's what I need.

And of course my husband Gary who believes in me, my mother who is well into her nineties and still proofs my work, and my brother who proudly leads my cheerleading squad and isn't shy about telling anyone that I'm an author. A bestselling author, he adds. I adore you three.

ABOUT THE AUTHOR

I started writing as a child, really. A few things happened on the way to becoming a published author ... specifically, a junior high school teacher who told me I couldn't write because I didn't want to study grammar.

That English teacher stopped my writing for years. But the muse couldn't be denied, and eventually I wrote, a lot, some of it award winning.

My husband told me repeatedly that independent publishing was becoming a valid way to publish a novel. I didn't believe him. I thought indie meant vanity press.

I couldn't have been more wrong.

I started pursuing this direction seriously, hit the keyboard, learned a litany of new things and published my first novel. My second book became a bestseller, and I'm absolutely on the right course in my life.

I live in Colorado with my husband Gary whom I met on a blind date—I can't imagine life without my best friend. We play in the mountains and travel as much as possible.

Find me at www.lasartor.com

DARE TO BELIEVE

BOOK ONE IN THE KAHUNA GROUP SERIES

CHAPTER ONE

THE MOVERS HAULED OUT THE LAST AND LARGEST PIECE OF THE furniture as Catherine Hemstead Malloy pushed the final suitcase into the rear of her old Subaru Outback, a remnant of her single days.

Scanning the small pile of boxes stacked near the moving truck, she decided it was time to get Haley and move on.

Cate had promised herself no looking back; onward was her new mantra. As soon as she drove out the imposing iron gates of the mansion her husband had named Highgate, she and her six-year-old daughter would begin their new life.

Tomorrow she started a society reporter's gig at the *Denver Post* and Haley started at day care. The mix-up over her interview at the *Los Angeles Star* newspaper ended all hope of getting a decent writing job, one that would actually pay her an almost living wage.

"Dude!" one of the movers cautioned.

Glancing over to the slate steps fronting Highgate's imposing doors, Cate saw Haley's armoire wobbling in the movers' grasp. The slighter of the duo struggled for balance on the lip of the chiseled stone step.

It took all her will power not to blurt out a "careful," knowing it would only earn her another complaint about the weight of the piece, and she was tired of their constant threats to escalate the price for moving the thing.

The heavy cherry wardrobe was Haley's choice of furniture to take with them to the new one-bedroom apartment. It held her toys, her clothes, and when she was younger, had been her favorite playhouse. It was the only furniture Haley wanted and, despite the ridiculously high cost of moving the thing, it was going to the minuscule apartment Cate had rented in Denver.

Watching as the two men navigated the remaining steps toward the decrepit truck parked near her ancient Subie, Cate appreciated the irony of the incongruous, even laughable, picture the vehicles made parked in front of the McMansion de Malloy. The huge pile of stone and plaster that had been the pride and joy of her late husband.

A new family was moving in soon, and Cate hoped this time the halls and rooms would be filled with laughter and love.

Fighting hard against the bitter memories worming into the already stressful day, Cate hurried around the perimeter of the house, aiming for the aspen grove where her daughter had begged to spend a last few minutes saying goodbye to her imaginary elfin friends. "Haley?"

Stepping into the empty clearing, Cate frowned at her daughter's disappearing act. "Haley? We've already gone through this. I promised we'd find another special garden in Denver. Your buds will come and play. I promise."

Nothing but silence answered her.

"Haley Marie Malloy, enough playing hide and seek! We're leaving. Now!"

Cate fought the tendril of remorse snaking through her soul. She rarely spoke to Haley in anything but calm tones. There hadn't really ever been the need to do otherwise, for her daughter, despite all the trauma she'd been through in the last six months, had never needed to be scolded. And if she needed five more minutes with her fairies and elfin friends, then, by God, Cate would give them to her.

Working hard to keep her pace slow, she walked the cedar path through the cool, dappled shade of the aspen grove, to the turquoise swimming pool and back again. Twice. Until her patience was burned through.

"Okay, baby, I'm sorry, but we really have to go." Moving deeper into the shady grove, sure Haley would jump out and try to scare her, Cate reached the high wall bordering the estate with no sign of her daughter.

About to retrace her steps back to the mansion, she stopped as a flash of pink caught her attention.

Hippity Hoppity Lippity Loppity, Haley's precious pink stuffed bunny, hung upside down on an aspen branch at the base of the wall.

Cate forgot to breathe.

It's okay, she's here somewhere. Just because Richard had died in a freak climbing accident six months ago didn't mean that something disastrous had happened to Haley. *Right. That's why you've been watching her like a hawk, because accidents* do *happen.* Even Luci, who sometimes babysat, was more alert now.

Pushing aside bushes, frantically checking the ground for any sign that her curious daughter might have tried to climb the wall and dropped Hippity, Cate saw only trampled leaves and a broken fern frond. The tree that snagged Hippity was too young, its branches too flimsy for even her rail-thin daughter to climb.

Cate grabbed Hippity, hugging the bunny tight. "Where's our girl, Hippity?"

A motor coughed and caught. The moving van! Maybe Haley had decided to play a trick on her mommy and hide in the armoire. The movers had certainly struggled with it.

The van was at the iron gates, ready to turn onto the county road as Cate rounded the corner of the mansion at a dead-on run. "Stop, wait! Stop!"

She sprinted down the long driveway, waving her arms. The wheezing of the ancient engine drowned her cries, and the van turned out of sight.

Cate backtracked and jumped into her car, throwing Hippity on the seat. The Subaru whined once, the ignition chattered, then silence. "Crap, crap, crap! Not now you pile of ..." She wrenched the key again. This time nothing but silence, not even the telltale chatter of a dead battery. *If only she'd kept the Range Rover ...* but thoughts like that were useless, there was no way she could keep up the expensive vehicle when it needed maintenance.

Reaching for her purse, she prayed the mover's phone number was on the manifest. "Thank you," she mumbled, shifting through gum wrappers, notes and lists for her cell phone.

It too was dead. Charging the battery had been the last thing on her mind. She threw the useless phone back into her bag.

Scrambling out of the car, Cate raced down the long winding driveway and onto the road. The truck was so far ahead.

Pushing her out-of-shape legs to pump faster, she ran down the center of the narrow road, frantically waving her arms. "Stop, dammit, stop."

∼

JASON ST. PIERRE PULLED SHARPLY INTO HIS DRIVEWAY AND skidded to a stop a mere inch from the wooden and iron gate as a woman running down the road, waving her arms, caught his eye.

Was that Cate? She was supposed to be gone by now, away from here.

Away from him.

He'd specifically stayed at his office in Denver to avoid any chance encounter, as the gates to her property and his faced each other on opposite sides of the county road. Drumming his fingers on the leather-wrapped steering wheel of the Tesla, he couldn't believe all his careful planning was for naught.

He punched in the gate's security code, convincing himself to drive on. Then, unable to resist, he looked down the road again. Cate—blonde hair flying, long tanned legs pumping, arms waving like a flying monkey—was chasing something.

Let her go. Let it go. Let it be done finally.

But he knew it wouldn't be done, he couldn't be healed until she was out of sight, not for a day or two, or even a week, but for good.

"Damn." Jason backed out and within seconds pulled alongside her. "Cate?" he yelled.

Let it go.

"Cate, what are you doing?" he yelled again.

She pointed in front of her.

He looked. The road was clear.

She slowed and finally stopped, bending over, breathing hard. He stopped the car beside her.

"Why are you running down the middle of the road?"

"Haley. Van. Stop it," she said between gasps.

"What?"

"Moving van. Haley."

He didn't understand what she was saying, but obviously something was seriously wrong. "We'll catch it, get in."

The Tesla's mighty horsepower made short work of the distance to the van. Jason laid on the horn with zero results. Waiting until they crested the hill and the road ahead was clear, he pulled even beside the van, only to hear the deep bass of hip hop blast from the windows.

Gunning the car, he pulled in front of them, turned the wheel hard and did a one-eighty.

The van squealed to a stop, running off the road onto the shoulder. "Dude, you crazy?" the driver yelled, swinging out from the cab, fists curled.

Jason met him before he took two steps. "We need you to open the back."

"Here? No way. Insurance."

"Please, my daughter may be playing a trick on me and hiding in the van," Cate said.

"There weren't no kids in the van when we locked it up."

"She'd be hiding in the armoire."

Silently, the men did as bid, then stood, arms crossed in annoyance, on either side of the ramp. Jason held out his hand, helping Cate up the steep metal incline.

He was stunned there was so little in the van. The house had been filled to the gills with furniture, art and knickknacks. Cate alone had enough clothes to fill this piece-of-junk van.

And why had she hired this company? Why not the best firm in Denver?

"Haley, you can come out, Mommy's not mad. I understand, baby."

Jason shot a glance at Cate, curious over the guilt lacing her voice.

They reached the armoire and Cate checked the left side, the open hanging area.

Empty. Absolutely empty, not even a hanger.

"I've got this side," he said. It was all drawers. He checked each one, knowing it was silly, but he had to make sure. He found a sketchpad in the bottom drawer and handed it to her.

Cate touched it softly, then tucked it in the gigantic leather satchel she carried.

"God, Jason, where is she? She'd never willingly leave Hippity behind."

"Let's get back to the house, check it carefully again, then if we can't find her—"

At her look of anguish, he amended his words. "Then we'll take it step by step. You can explain everything to me on the drive back."

She nodded, then swayed.

Grabbing her, he put his arm around her waist. Damn, she still fit perfectly against him. "Have you eaten today?"

"A banana."

He went down the ramp before her, holding her hand, just in case she had another dizzy spell. They headed toward the Tesla.

"Hey, what about this junk?" the van driver asked.

"Take it—"

"Take it to the apartment." Cate interrupted, fished in her pocket for a second, then pulled out a set of old and worn keys, unclipped one and handed it to the mover. "Just put it all in there, lock the door, and give Barbara, the manager, the key."

"We need you to sign."

"Do it. She can sign later," Jason ordered, giving them an icy glare. It had them moving fast. They shoved in the ramps, locked the door and were on their way by the time he got Cate into his car.

"I'm really worried, Jason. What if she ran away?" Cate said and started chewing her nails.

Images of a little blonde girl with green eyes and a sunny smile flashed before him as he drove toward a house he'd never wanted to enter again.

∾

JASON WAS GOOD TO HIS WORD. EVEN AS HE PAINSTAKINGLY searched through every cabinet and closet, nook and niche, Cate knew the house was empty. The connection she always felt around Haley was severed, a queasy emptiness in its place.

She followed slowly as he scanned inside the Thai-inspired pool house and through meticulously designed gardens—the Zen tea house in the Japanese garden, the playhouse cabin in the miniature forest, the calm aspen meadow.

Haley wasn't on the property.

Now, back at the front of the house, sitting on the topmost slate step in the shade of the stone portico, Cate fought full-on nausea. She had no one to turn to, no family, no friends. It hadn't mattered when she was single. All decisions she made affected her and only her. She'd learned the lesson of independence young and learned it well.

But Haley's disappearance wasn't something she could handle alone. And as much as she dreaded asking for help from the police, Jason, at her request, was now on the phone to Chief Anders.

Cate glanced at her former lover standing by his sleek red car, a deep furrow of concentration carved between his brows as he talked on his cell.

For an instant, the years fled, and she wasn't alone, the memory of him as he lay beside her, listening intently to her plans, with the same creases marring his brow. She'd reached up to smooth them away and he took her hand, kissed each finger ... then as quickly as the memory came, the solace of it fled.

Six years and a chasm of pain separated them, and frankly, she didn't have the foggiest idea why he'd bothered now to help her this much.

They weren't on speaking terms, civil only at functions where air kissing was the norm and you *darling*-ed your way through the party.

Jason never air kissed. He stood apart from that kind of phony cordiality. When she'd been on his arm, she'd admired his strength of avoiding pretenses. And when she was no longer a part of his life, she protected herself from the ache of his indifference by pretending he was an arrogant jerk.

The truth was Jason was a protector of those whom he thought needed protection and guidance. *Even if they didn't need or want his guidance.* These were traits Cate realized about him after the fact. And for most people these were admirable qualities, for how could anyone not want a protector, a defender, a guide? *Unless his way was the only way.*

She looked at him again, talking on the phone, making things happen, and bit her lip, knowing she wasn't being fair; he was helping because of Haley.

Jason's very strengths allowed him to be gentle and the champion of the innocent.

After Richard died, Jason hadn't minded when her daughter wanted to visit and play secretary with Luci, Jason's business assistant. Nor when Luci babysat. Or when Mark, Jason's live-in jack-of-all-trades, offered her a ride on the golf cart to the village store. And even when Marta, Jason's trusted confidante, allowed Haley to cook with her. They all got along great. *It's only you Jason doesn't want to be around.*

She walked over to her useless car. Grabbing Hippity off the seat, she held the bunny close. "Hippity? I wish you could tell me what happened to our girl."

She gently shook the bunny, then paused as a familiar scent wafted off the stuffed animal.

Sniffing harder, she shook the bunny again, trying to place the scent, but nothing would surface.

"Anders is meeting us at my place," Jason said.

Cate startled, so focused on placing the scent that it took her a second to realize what Jason meant. "Your place? I'm not leaving Highgate. What if Haley comes back? She'll be hungry and probably scared. I'm not leaving."

"You have no electricity, water or phone. Mark is coming over to be here—"

"Mark?"

"He volunteered. He's bringing an air mattress, a cooler of food, including Haley's favorite PBJ's, and several battery lanterns."

"Perfect. Have him bring two air mattresses. And Anders can meet me here."

They stood toe to toe. Jason's jaw worked. She needed to make him understand. "I know she was upset over the move, but I ... we couldn't stay here any longer. I thought she understood."

"It's pretty hard for a six-year-old to understand anything like that."

Guilt ate deeper into her hearing him vocalize exactly what she knew in her heart. She could rationalize leaving the only home her daughter had ever known until the moon turned blue, but that didn't mean squat to Haley. This was home. This was where she played with her daddy. This was safe and loving, at least for Haley. She and Richard had made sure Haley knew they adored her... if not each other.

"Cate, the second she shows, Mark will call, and we'll be here in under a minute. But we need to get some food into you, or else you know what happens."

He held the car door open for her.

Her head did feel two sizes too big, and she had the shakes, yet she couldn't leave. "Mark can bring another sandwich," she said, knowing she was being stubborn, but not unreasonable. She needed to hold Haley the second she came back and it only made the nightmare worse to see Mark driving up in the golf cart, loaded with supplies. "I can't leave here. I can't abandon her."

"I'll keep the door open and a light burning so she'll know someone is here," Mark offered. "Hey, give me the bunny, it'll make her happy until you get here."

Still she couldn't take a step toward Jason's car.

"Compromise, Cate."

His words were a slap in the face. Compromise was exactly what she'd asked Jason to do six years ago. He hadn't heard her then ... or maybe he had, since he threw the words back at her now. But he hadn't learned.

Slowly she handed the bunny to Mark.

Ignoring Jason's hand, she got into the car and it began to roll forward. "It'd help if you turned the car on."

His laughter rang out, rubbing her ire into high gear. "Cate, it's electric, a Tesla. No engine noise."

She felt his glance and turned to meet it, sobered by the worry she saw, mirroring her own.

He reached toward her cheek, then lowered his hand.

Relieved and saddened, Cate looked the other way as Jason accelerated through the gears.

DRIVING THROUGH THE WROUGHT IRON GATES OF HIGHGATE WAS A relief. The gates were as their name proclaimed: high, imposing and slightly gaudy, at least to Jason's eye. They were also a daily physical reminder of who lived behind them.

The short drive to his house was simply crossing the county road. And usually, when he drove through his gates, he entered his sanctuary.

The long drive lined with blue spruce and aspen ironed out the stresses of the day. Lush mountain ferns grew naturally, and lichen-covered boulders lay where they'd landed. Nothing was placed strategically by landscapers.

He had gardeners, just like the Malloys, but his crew, led by Mark, understood the land and the mountain he lived on. They worked *with* nature, not against it. The Malloy team transformed the grounds of Highgate into something completely artificial.

Today, with Cate beside him, the drive was not calming. He didn't want her in his house. He didn't want memories of them racing laps in his pool to haunt him—again. He didn't want her lemony and verbena perfume to linger anywhere—again.

But Haley was missing, and he'd do anything for the miniature of Cate. Haley should have been their child. And while he completely distrusted her mother, he'd cut off his arm before he'd risk harm coming to her daughter.

Chief Anders's siren split the air.

Jason had left the gates open, and the white Morrison Colorado Police cruiser pulled in right behind him in the broad circular drive fronting his home.

The front door opened, and Marta stood waiting in the deep, cool shade of the foyer. Marta was the only "family" he had. She'd been his aunt's right hand "man" and a financial whiz in her own right. She'd retired when his aunt died and stayed with him when not traveling. She'd been there through the "Cate" period. To Jason, Marta was his sixty-year-young ally, the only person he really trusted.

He followed Cate into the foyer, then glanced back at Anders, who looked around at everything quickly, as if making mental notes. Always the investigator.

"Marta, do you mind making us some coffee and sandwiches?" Jason asked.

She shook her head, then without any hesitation, hugged Cate. "Oh, honey, Mark told me about Haley. Don't worry, we'll find her. We all love our little Haley."

Jason kept his gaze glued to the floor as Cate dashed away sudden tears.

"We'll be in the office," he said, a bit more gruffly than intended.

Cate settled into the club chair she'd always preferred. Jason sat behind his teak desk, needing the barrier it provided. And Chief Anders paced until Marta brought a tray of sandwiches and two carafes of coffee.

She offered the platter first to Cate. "Okay, honey, now you eat. You have to keep strong, and you don't want any nasty ole migraine to get in the way," Marta chided.

To Jason's surprise, Cate did as Marta bade, even biting into the thick bread and chicken salad before Marta had offered the platter to the chief.

The chief refused.

Marta placed the platter on the desk and poured coffee for Cate and Jason.

Anders cleared his throat, looking at Cate. "Do you mind if we go through this while you eat?"

Cate shook her head, then put her sandwich down. Jason could have strangled the chief, making it sound trivial to eat at a time like this. But then the man didn't know Cate like he did.

Anders nodded to Jason. "St. Pierre filled me in, Mrs. Malloy. Said you've checked the grounds, the house and the moving van, correct?"

At Cate's short nod, he continued. "And apparently a special toy was left behind?"

Cate nodded again. "Hippity. A stuffed pink rabbit that goes everywhere with Haley."

"Has your daughter ever run away before?"

"Never!" Cate stood abruptly, spilling her coffee. She banged the cup on the table and stared at Anders. Her mouth worked, but she uttered nothing, and Jason watched as she took a breath, then another in an effort to calm herself. "But this move has been hard on her," she admitted.

"You didn't find any kind of note or Mommy letter or—"

"Damn! Haley's sketchpad." Cate smacked her forehead with the palm of her hand.

"I'll get it." Jason bolted from the room.

He was back in a flash with the sketchpad held between thumb and forefinger, and put it on the desk. "We found it in the armoire, bottom drawer."

Cate reached for the pad.

"Stop. Fingerprints." Anders used the sterling letter opener lying on the desk to turn back the cover. "Let me know if anything about the drawings looks peculiar or out of context in Haley's life." He flipped the pages after Cate studied each one.

Jason saw a family of three on the paper. Three blond heads atop stick figures having a picnic or playing in the playhouse. Richard, Cate and Haley. A few pages later, there were two blond heads. Haley and her mommy. She must have recently drawn that picture. Richard died only six months ago.

"Wait, go back a page."

Jason jerked back to the present as Anders obliged.

"This is odd."

"Why?" Anders asked.

"Haley's never drawn anybody but her daddy and me with her."

Jason saw it immediately. Haley was holding hands with a dark-haired woman. Beside them, Haley had drawn what looked to be a suitcase.

"Who does she know with dark hair?

Dare To Believe

www.ingramcontent.com/pod-product-compliance
Lightning Source LLC
Chambersburg PA
CBHW050044180626
46810CB00002B/887